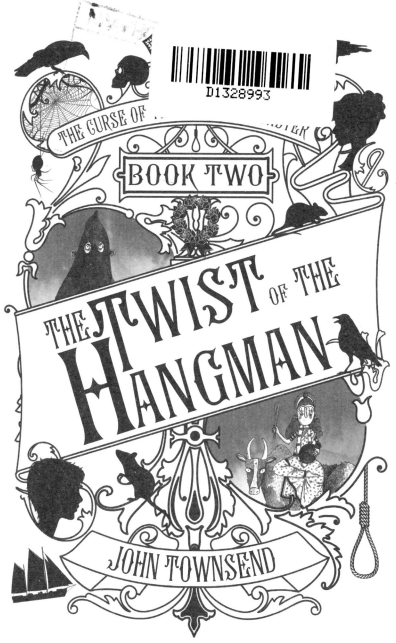

THE CURSE OF ... ...TER

BOOK TWO

THE TWIST OF THE HANGMAN

JOHN TOWNSEND

SCRIBO

a SALARIYA imprint

For the first ten years of my life I had nothing. Nothing at all in the world. And when you've got nothing in the world, you've got nothing in the world to lose. Apart from your life, of course... and I was ready to take the risk rather than do nothing. I was ready to risk anything. I was ready to risk losing life itself.

But then, surprisingly, something special came into my possession. I also acquired something that no one could ever take away. I learned to read. A new world opened up to me... and I uncovered a secret beyond my dreams. For the first time I glimpsed light, colour and truth in a dark, dismal, diseased age.

There was a time when it was dangerous to be a child. There was a time when no one dared tell their story. Now is the time to tell mine.

Cephas Catchpole

Summary of Book 1:

GRAVEROBBERS AND GALLOWS

Cephas Catchpole is just another orphan struggling to survive in a shadowy England just over 200 years ago. All he knows is that his mother died giving birth to him – and his distraught father died a few years later from the dreaded smallpox. No one understood why Cephas escaped the epidemic that claimed so many. Growing up in the parish workhouse, Cephas, at just eight years old, was apprenticed to Artimus Groundling, a mean chimney sweep. After two years, everything changes when two accidents happen – both on the same day…

1. While scrambling up a chimney, Cephas discovers a stone jar hidden behind some bricks. It contains something both sinister and assuring, starting him wondering and giving him hope. But he also discovers a strange girl locked in a room, closeted away from the outside world.

2. While trying to escape from the evil Dr Mordecai

Brimstone, Cephas falls badly and is knocked unconscious. Not willing to pay for treatment, Artimus plies him with gin and laudanum, rendering Cephas so lifeless as to be promptly buried in a makeshift coffin in a pauper's grave.

Dug up by a couple of ruffian body-snatchers (Jack Cutpurse and Horace Dalrymple), Cephas is recruited into their nocturnal graveyard shenanigans and the murky world of street crime, public hangings and grotesque medicine. One of Cephas's sinister missions is to squeeze through the gates at the prison courtyard for two prized items from the gallows: a piece of hangman's rope and the hand of a hanged man. While cowering under the scaffold, Cephas finds something belonging to the hangman. Something to cause a bizarre twist...

Cephas is now on the run – desperate to find answers.

April

eing alive came as an amazing surprise. Being free seemed extraordinary.

Landing in the street from a window early in the morning, I ran off with my feet pounding a thrilling rhythm, 'I'm running away, I'm running away, I'm running away…'

After my narrow escape from the grave, I felt luck was at last on my side – to be escaping again and free from fearful adults for the first time in my life. Although the den of thieves plotting gruesome crimes was now behind me, I feared my chances of staying free were slim, and of surviving for long even slimmer. My new-found freedom meant I was totally alone in the world. Alone, homeless and penniless. At ten years old and unable to read or write, I knew that keeping safe in this dangerous wide world would be my biggest challenge yet.

Like a lost soul, I wandered aimlessly through the empty grey streets of the city. Soon I came to where the market had been a bustling rumpus the day before. Now the street was strewn with filth and debris, like the aftermath of a battle. Mud and dung squelched underfoot and the air was thick with vile odours. Heaps of ragged children sprawled in doorways and across the steps of public houses, like the slain. They crawled between battered boxes and crates, some sleeping inside them or huddled under stinking sacks. Most of these poor specimens looked dazed, diseased or deformed and I knew only too well this was where I would end up if I didn't find a way to survive. I vowed never to end up like these hopeless souls. The streets were just too dangerous, especially as I now risked being kidnapped or worse by those from whom I'd just escaped.

Nagging questions whirred around my head and I just didn't know where I should begin to find answers. I turned around and headed away, knowing for certain that I had to escape the city, leaving my past behind. Eventually I came to the churchyard where I'd cowered in terror just nights before and where I'd once been buried in a coffin. Being pronounced dead by the loathsome Doctor Mordecai Brimstone and declared an expired orphan chimney sweep had left me haunted by this place. But it mysteriously drew me back, as if to prove I really had escaped the grave. The gates were open and, as the sun rose above the flowering shrubs, this no longer seemed like the fearful place I dreaded. I walked inside and sat alone to think of my future, among familiar statues towering above me on their granite plinths. With sunlight and birdsong, this was as good a place as any to plan where I could go and what my life might be like now. It was a life I was grateful I still clung to. I looked across to where I'd been buried and was amazed to see a wreath of daffodils and tulips. I went over for a closer look, when I heard a voice behind me.

'What are you doing?' It was a man with a grey beard and straggly white hair, dressed in a long muddy coat. He was leaning on a spade and was clearly the grave-digger.

'I've just come to look at this grave,' I said.

'Know him, did yer?'

'Yes.'

'So you'll know he was Artimus Groundling's young chimney sweep. I buried him a few weeks back.'

'Who put the flowers there?' I asked.

'Don't know who she was. She asked me where young Catchpole was buried so I showed her. She said she'd signed the book in the church. I never know all the comings and goings here. Just as well, what with some of the night-time capers in these parts.'

'Do you mind if I sit here for a while?'

'So long as you don't fall in any fresh holes!' He laughed wheezily and waddled away to trim a hedge. I sat in the warm sunshine by the angel statue where I'd previously felt so miserable and where I'd traced letters in the marble – and I promised myself that somehow, whatever it took, I'd learn to read and try to do something with my life. I never wanted to get tangled in crime or midnight body-snatching again.

For the first time, I could safely take from my pocket the hangman's pendant I'd found under the gallows and look at it closely. Engraved in the gold was exactly the same picture as the one tattooed on my wrist – a smiling woman sitting on an animal. I examined it carefully and wondered for a long time.

Two words were engraved around the edge of the pendant and I knew the first letter to be an 'S'. I was sure the words were the same as those on the pot I'd found hidden up a chimney in Brimstone House; a pot with the very same image. As far as I knew, the pot was still in Edith Brimstone's locked room, where the vile doctor kept his daughter prisoner. Being certain that the clue to who I was and to the guiding voice in my head had something to do with that picture of 'My Lady', I was determined to find answers once and for all.

Horrifying though the idea of returning to Brimstone House seemed, I so much wanted to see the girl called Edith and her mother again. I felt sorry for them locked in their rooms and I knew they'd meant me no harm. I wanted to let them know I was alive and well, as well as ask questions.

But there were serious risks if I returned. I daren't meet Doctor Brimstone or his housekeeper Mrs Quilter again. They would surely beat me – yet, if they were of the firm belief I was dead, they were hardly likely to be expecting me. So I stood up, put the pendant back in my pocket and walked from the churchyard. I had no clue where Brimstone House was, but I had a good idea of how I could get there. That would mean taking a considerable risk. 'My Lady' smiled up at me from my wrist. I'd survived a lot so far, so I quietly asked her to keep protecting me from whatever dangers lay ahead.

By mid-afternoon, I was outside Gryme Street Hospital, watching the comings and goings of horses and carriages. I sat on the steps opposite the main entrance for a long time until I saw Doctor Brimstone walk out through the main doors, carrying a case and wearing a hat and frock coat. As he headed towards a waiting carriage, I ran across the street, making sure I kept well out of his sight. He barked something at the coachman and clambered up into the carriage. As soon as he was inside, I ran up behind, just as the horse began moving off. Although I'd often seen other children clinging onto the back of carriages for a free ride, I'd never tried it myself, and I knew I risked being whipped by any passing coachmen on the street. I quickly got a foothold on the back and clung on with my fingers, even though my arms were soon aching as the street rumbled beneath me. As the horse trotted over cobbles and the carriage wheels clattered and jolted, I managed to climb onto a luggage rack where I felt more secure with the increasing speed. I watched the busy streets disappear behind us as we clopped on past lines of dilapidated houses like the one I'd left that morning. Soon the carriage was rumbling along between grander houses and tree-lined streets until we entered parkland and leafy avenues. Sweeping through grand gates, we crunched up a gravel drive, which I recognised to be the one I'd once walked with Master Groundling when clutching my chimney brushes. The coachman shouted 'Wooa!' and the horse slowed to a steady walk as we swung round in front of the house and scrunched to a halt. I leapt off the back and crouched under the carriage.

Doctor Brimstone stepped down onto the gravel as the carriage-springs creaked above me. 'Be here tomorrow morning at seven o'clock,' he grunted before crunching away up the steps and entering the grand front door. As soon as the wheels turned beside me, I darted behind one of the entrance pillars before creeping off round the side of the house, keeping my head well below the windows. By the back kitchen, I knew there was a laundry room where sheets were hung to dry, with the door always left open to catch the breeze. I slipped inside, headed down a tunnel of sheets and climbed the steps up to a door. I put my ear to the keyhole and listened. There were no voices so, slowly lifting the latch and pushing the door, I poked my head into a narrow hallway, where I heard the tinkle of teaspoons in saucers coming from the kitchen. There was no one to be seen so I hurtled down the hall to a door at the end, which I knew opened into a study. Once inside the musty, book-lined room, I headed straight to the empty fireplace. I remembered climbing up this chimney before, shortly before all the fires had been lit throughout the house to smoke me out. I was thankful that no fires were burning now, having checked for signs of smoke from the chimneys when scanning the roof as I arrived. Luckily the day was too warm for fires… yet.

I knew many of the chimneys were connected to

each other and one of the side vents dropped into the hearth in Edith's room. My problem now was to remember how the maze of pitch-black tunnels linked up. As I scrambled up, down and along, I came to where I thought I'd first heard Edith's sobs drifting up from her room. I groped around and sure enough, my fingers found the tiny recess where I'd discovered the engraved stone pot. Slowly I began to descend the chimney towards a grey patch of light below. I inched my way down, trying not to make a sound, until I stood, at last, in the hearth and peered out into the room. Alone in front of the window at a table sat a girl with dark hair tied in green ribbons, doing a jigsaw puzzle. She was humming quietly to herself and was oblivious to me stepping out into her bedroom.

Fearing I would startle Edith into hysterical shrieking that would announce my presence to everyone in the house, I simply whispered, 'Good day, Edith.'

She turned suddenly, her eyes opening wide and her eyebrows raised. With a startled gulp, she clasped her throat and whimpered.

'Please don't be frightened,' I tried to reassure her. 'It's me, Cephas. I didn't die when I fell from your mother's window and I've come back to see you.'

She sat motionless, the colour draining from her face.

'Please don't faint,' I said, taking a step nearer. 'I would have come back earlier but...'

I stopped when I saw her shoulders shaking and tears spilling down her cheeks. She struggled to speak, fiddling with a piece of jigsaw before mumbling, 'It can't be you. I saw you in the coffin. I put you in a shirt and placed a rose in your hands. Are you a ghost?'

'No, I'm real. I'm really sorry to upset you.' By now I was sobbing, too. She stood up, took a step forward and touched me.

'I just don't understand,' she said. 'It doesn't make sense. How did you get in here?'

I gabbled the full story of my last few weeks and of how I was desperate to find answers. I told her how I sensed a voice inside me, like my father guiding me. I knew nothing about him and longed to find out who he was. I told her I felt certain her mother must have known him by the way she'd reacted when I'd told her my name.

'I'm just like your jigsaw,' I blurted in frustration, 'only I can't find the pieces and none of them will ever fit together. Please help me put together just a bit of the picture so I can get a glimpse of who I am.'

'All I know is,' Edith said, still dabbing at her eyes, 'my father knew your father but he won't talk about him. If I ask, he ignores me or flies into a rage.'

'He was certainly mad about the picture of "My Lady" on the pot I found. I keep wondering who she is.'

Edith looked closely at my tattooed wrist. 'Yes, like I told you before, she's just like the face carved in the bark of my father's dragon flower tree. Cephas, I can't believe you've come back. I was so sad when you fell from Mama's window. I've been upset for weeks. You can't believe how pleased I am to see you.'

'I knew you must have been upset. Was it you who put the rose in my hands?'

'Yes. I asked the gardener to put a rose on your grave each week. He has to grow blooms all through the winter in the glasshouse. My father insists that rose petals keep away disease so we always have roses here.'

'Well you don't have to bother putting any more on the grave! I saw the latest wreath of flowers only this morning. Daffodils and tulips.'

'Wreath of flowers? Daffodils?'

'Thank you for sending them, even though I was alive and well!'

She looked at me straight in the eyes and smiled for the first time. 'You must have another girlfriend. They weren't from here. We don't grow daffodils. The last single rose I sent was over a week ago.'

The dragon flower tree

—— *Chapter 2* ——

dith snapped a piece of jigsaw into place, completing the bottom edge of the puzzle, before grinning triumphantly. 'Things soon start to make sense after you get the corners and edges. That's where we must start with you and we'll piece together who you are. We'll firstly try to find out when and where you were born.'

'I've no idea,' I answered. 'All I know is, I was

born about ten years ago somewhere round here. My father was a gardener called Cornelius. My mother never saw me. That's all I know.'

Edith looked out of the window and sighed. 'Sometimes puzzles don't turn out as you think they will. You might find out something bad or horrible. Are you sure you want to take the risk?'

'I'm getting used to risks,' I said. 'I know getting to the truth might be painful but never knowing the truth at all will be like spending the rest of my life stuck up that chimney. Even if my parents didn't love me or if they did terrible things, I still want to know something about them.'

She didn't look convinced. 'I know who my father is, but I still don't know much about him. The sad part is, I don't want to. I just don't care. That must sound terrible but it's true. That's because he doesn't care about Mama and me at all. All he thinks about is money… and that horrible Mrs Quilter.'

She looked out through the window again, as if the answers to all our problems and questions were just beyond the trees. I changed the subject and hoped to persuade her to help with something else.

'I think I can remember being taught to read once but I just can't make sense of all those strange marks on the page. I'd love to read. I'd be able to find out so much more if I could read for myself. I never had the chance to learn at the workhouse. Do you think you could teach me, Edith?'

I waited for a reaction and after no more than a moment's thought, she giggled. 'It will be my pleasure! My first job will be to teach you all the letters and their sounds…'

She suddenly froze at the rattle of a key in the door. Within seconds I was clambering back up the chimney, as the door opened and feet strode into the room. I immediately recognised the voice to be her father's.

'Now, Edith, what have you learned today?'

'I've been reading.'

'What about?'

'Trees.'

'Trees?'

'But I can't find anything about the dragon flower tree. Like the one in the garden. Why did you bring it back from India, father?'

'It wasn't my idea. It's an ugly thing, anyway. One of my companions wanted to bring it back. They said it might be useful for medicine. Hogwash if you ask me. Gullible twaddle.'

Edith paused before asking the big question. 'So why is there a carving of a lady on its bark?'

'It's just superstition,' he shouted, 'it's nothing to do with real science. A lot of nonsensical nincompoopery. So stop all these silly questions. It's just a tree and that's all there is to it.'

'Then tell me about India, father. What's it like?'

'Hot and dusty.'

'It must have been exciting to sail all that way.'

'Not at all. It was full of death and disease.'

'Why did you go?'

'To bring back things to help me in my work.'

'Who went with you?'

'Someone I'd prefer to forget so no more questions. Show me your jigsaw.'

'There's just one last question, father. Then I'll ask no more. Please can I ask you?'

There was a long pause and a sigh. 'Very well, what is it?'

'Who was Cornelius Catchpole? I think our gardener mentioned the name.'

I held my breath and waited for a burst of anger or a stamp of his foot. Instead I had to strain to hear his surprisingly quiet reply.

'I do not wish to hear that name. However, I will

tell you one thing but after that I never want that name spoken in this house again. He and I went to India together but we didn't agree on many things. He even dared to try and stop my work when we returned. If he'd had his way, I wouldn't have this splendid house today. I'd have ended up as just another poor country doctor – like him.'

'He was a doctor? I thought he was a gardener.'

'He called himself a botanist. He grew and studied plants for medicine. A waste of time if you ask me. Rose petals are all we need. It was his idea to go to India as a missionary but I told him that wouldn't make him rich. I was right, too. He died without a penny to his name. There, that's all there is to it and I never want to hear you mention such things again. I'll be back in an hour to bid you goodnight.'

I heard his footsteps clump across the floor, followed by the door being locked behind him. Only then did I feel it was safe to descend once more. Edith sat smiling. 'Did you hear any of that? By the look on your face you did!'

I was thrilled. 'My father was a doctor! He was a botanist! He was a missionary in India! I had no idea. I've just learned more about him in a few seconds than in all my life.'

'So it looks as if we've just found a few pieces of your jigsaw, Cephas. And I can be certain we'll find a few more soon. All it will take is a little talk with my mother. Before long we might just fit together the bottom edge of Cephas Catchpole's life. But until then, I think it's time for your first reading lesson…'

It was late and the darkening sky was already sprinkled with starlight. I looked up at the moon from Edith's window. 'I seem to have got to know the moon very well lately. We're like close friends. It feels good to be in its company for once without being up to my neck in mischief and skulduggery. Last night…' It was only then I realised it was just the night before I'd been skulking at the gallows. No wonder I was now so tired. I hadn't eaten all day, either.

'Any chance of some food and sleep? If not, I'll die for real and you'll have to bury me all over again.'

Edith didn't smile. 'Please don't say that. That day was terrible. I'd never forgive myself if anything happened to you again. You must take great care here. I'll get you some food and think about where you can sleep – somewhere no one will find you.' She reached out and pulled a cord hanging from the wall. 'Sorry, but you'll have to hide again.'

'What is that?' I asked, intrigued.

'It rings a bell in the kitchen. Mrs Quilter or one of the maids will arrive shortly. Would you like some bread and cold sausage?'

I laughed. 'I think I'm turning into a sausage! Thank you, that would be good. And a glass of milk, please.' I disappeared once more up the chimney as footsteps approached and I heard Edith asking for supper. Sure enough, within minutes, a tray of food and a glass of milk appeared. I was astounded. 'I can't believe it,' I said as I stepped back down into the hearth. 'You can have whatever you want at the pull of a rope.'

Her eyes looked very sad. 'No,' she sighed. 'Not whatever I want at all.'

While I ate ravenously, Edith opened the window and peered outside. There was a distant rumble of thunder as a warm breeze stirred the trees. She pondered for a while. 'I wonder if Josiah ever knew your father. He's our gardener and he's been here for years, since long before I was born. He's a friendly old man and I'm sure he'll talk to you.

His potting shed is just behind that wall at the end of the lawn. He keeps it clean and tidy and it will be safe for you to sleep in there. I can give you a blanket. The only thing is, you'll have to climb out of this window. Please don't fall again.'

'I wouldn't have fallen before if your father hadn't grabbed me,' I said.

She pointed to a ledge. 'There's plenty to grab hold of and it's not far down.'

I dropped the blanket onto the flowerbed below as Edith sighed, 'I've never risked climbing out on my own. There are times when I've longed to get out of here… and run. I'm going to watch how you do it and maybe soon…'

The clouds were rolling across the moon by the time I was scrambling down the ivy under Edith's window. She called down, 'I'll be waiting for you tomorrow with some breakfast.' I landed on the blanket, picked it up and hurried off across the lawn as the first spots of rain fell. By the time I found the potting shed and its door handle in the dark, streaks of lightning lit up the sky. Tumbling inside, I slammed the door behind me. From what I could see in the flashes, it was quite cosy inside, not that I really cared. I would have slept anywhere.

I was soon lying in a pile of straw, oblivious to the hammering rain and crashing thunder. Sleep had never been so welcome and I closed my eyes with a proud smile because, at last, I'd discovered my father had been a clever man of medicine. What's more, for the first time ever, I could sleep without fearing those around me and at last I even knew how to write my very own name.

I was woken by what sounded like tapping. As I opened my eyes and smelt straw and onions, I thought I was back with Master Groundling. The onions were strung around the walls of the shed, the door was half open and the tapping was a steady dripping of water from the roof into a bucket.

'Quite a storm it was, 'an all.'

I sat up, squinting to see where the voice was coming from. An old man sat on an upturned barrel, planting seeds in a pot.

'Not that it seemed to trouble you at all. Slept right through it, you did. The rain's done a drop of good to them seed potatoes and radishes, I'm glad to say. You should have seen the rain first thing. It was wet enough for a walking stick.'

He chuckled and hummed a tune to himself.

'I hope you don't mind me being here,' I said. 'Edith said it would be all right.'

'Did she now?'

'She said you were a kind and friendly gentleman. That's if you're the gardener.'

He snorted as he laughed. 'Well I'm not exactly the lord of the manor, am I? Yes, I'm Josiah Brimble, if that's what you mean. 'And who might you be?'

'My name's Cephas,' I said. I leaned forward to look at him closely as I added, 'Cephas Catchpole.'

'Catchpole? Surely you're not…'

'My father was Cornelius Catchpole. Did you know him?'

The man stood up, wiped his hand down his smock and shook me by the hand vigorously.

'The kindest gentleman I ever had the fortune to know.' Before he'd finished shaking my hand, I burst into tears and I threw my arms around this total stranger. He didn't seem too bothered by my outburst as he patted me on the head.

'A lot of the flowers in these gardens were from Doctor Catchpole. Foxgloves that he used to help cure the dropsy. There was nothing he didn't know about all kinds of plants. He used many to treat the sick. A lot of the mixtures he made were for the dreaded pox. It was such a tragedy that he couldn't cure himself. He caught the worst sort, so they do say.'

Josiah sat down with a grunt and picked up a tray of seeds from the bench. I could now see his face more clearly, with its mass of white whiskers and ruddy, purple-veined cheeks, topped by a thread-bare hat with frayed edges. 'See these seeds,' he said. 'These came from your father's stock. They be marigolds, the herb of the sun, as he called them. Together with saffron, these have been used as a remedy of the measles and smallpox for years. Your father used the juice of marigold leaves mixed with vinegar, and any hot swelling bathed with it was instantly eased. He once administered it to my troublesome knees and did them the power of good. And he made no charge, either. The marigold flowers he used in broths or as a tea were to comfort the heart and spirits. I've known him make a poultice with the dry flowers in powder, hog's-grease, turpentine and rosin, and apply to the breast to strengthen and give succour to many a feverish heart – mine included. Yes, he was a fine physician and the gentlest of gentlemen. A Godly man, if I may say so. One of life's saints.'

I didn't want this old man to stop telling me what I'd longed to hear. However, I interrupted him with the other question uppermost in my mind. 'What about my mother? Did you know her?'

He thought for a while. 'I can't say I did. I heard about what happened to her. Very sad. They lived in a village a few miles away. Come with me and I'll show you Doctor Catchpole's special tree.'

'I'd better not come outside yet. You see, Doctor Brimstone won't be happy if he sees me here.'

'Well Doctor Brimstone ain't going to see yer, is he? He's at the hospital. It's mid-afternoon!'

I had no idea I'd slept for so long and as I emerged from the shed into a warm, steamy afternoon, I looked across at the house surrounded by beautiful gardens. As Josiah led the way across the lawns and past all colours of rhododendron bushes, I saw Edith running barefoot towards us.

'I managed to get out! My governess left my door unlocked.'

'Don't you get into trouble, Miss Brimstone,' Josiah called, doffing his hat.

'I don't care,' she squealed. 'I'm free!'

We stood beneath a tree with sacks tied over the ends of its branches. 'As soon as the threat of frost passes, I'll take off the sacks and this tree will have lovely white flowers,' Josiah announced proudly.

'That's why it's called a white dragon tree,' Edith added. 'Each flower's a bit like a tiny dragon.'

'It has many names,' Josiah went on, 'like tiger tongue and corkwood, but your good father called it *sesbania formosa*. It was only a sapling when he planted it. He told me the people in India used the juice from the flowers to treat headaches and stuffy noses. But, and this is why he brought it back, he said the bark can be steeped in hot water and drunk to ease the smallpox. That's why some of the bark is missing. And just here is a carving of a lady on a cow.'

'I told you,' Edith said to me. 'It's just the same as the face on that pot and on your wrist.'

Josiah examined the buds on the lower twigs. 'As far as I know, she's meant to be some sort of Indian goddess who protects people from smallpox. I believe her name means "the cool one" as she is said to bring down the fever. That carving in the bark was done by an Indian gentleman. He told me

33

it stopped Mrs Brimstone dying from the disease. I sent some to your father with Doctor Brimstone but sadly it arrived too late to save him.'

I touched the tree and held on to it, stroking its bark. This was the first contact I'd had with anything connected with my father.

'Thank you for telling me all this, Mr Brimble. It's a great help to me.'

'It's my pleasure, Master Catchpole. And if I may say so, you have your father's looks about you. If you turn out as half as good a person as your father, you'll be a fine man.'

I shook him by the hand again, as the tears rose in my eyes.

'I suppose you've already had words with Nellie Hawksworthy, have you?' he asked.

'Who's that?'

'Mrs Hawksworthy was your father's housekeeper for a while. I can't be sure where she lives these days but I'll see if I can find out for you. She knew him well.'

I thanked him again, before Edith led me away towards the house. 'I've told Mama you're here and she's thrilled you're alive and well. She wants to meet you again but she's worried in case Mrs

Quilter sees you so we'd better creep up the back stairs. You must be hungry so I've collected lots of nice things from the kitchen. Not a sausage in sight! Father has an anatomy demonstration so he'll be late home, which means we don't have to hurry.'

We entered a side door and climbed two flights of stairs, then tiptoed across a landing before Edith tapped on her mother's door, turned the key and we both went inside. The room was just as I remembered and her mother sat in the same rocking chair, her face covered by a veil. 'Cephas,' she began, holding out her hand for me to touch, 'I cannot begin to tell you how sad we've been here after your terrible fall. I should never have told you to climb from this window. Please forgive me. Let me touch you and know that you really are alive.'

I held her hand and she stroked my arm. 'May I touch your face? I'll be gentle. It's my way of knowing who you are.' Her fingertips brushed over my nose, chin and cheeks. 'A kind face, I would say. You don't smell so much of soot this time,' she said, 'more like straw and onions. Now, please eat the food on the tray.'

Once more I ate heartily and soon finished a plate of barley porridge with mutton, two hard boiled duck eggs, bread with butter, cheese and a handful of Josiah's radishes. Edith chatted away about piecing together my life's jigsaw when her mother observed, 'I am very impressed by your manners, Cephas. Who taught you not to speak with your mouth full?'

I stopped to think. 'I've no idea. All meals had to be eaten in silence at the workhouse.'

'I think it was your father. I remember he was very well-mannered and gracious, always thoughtful of others. A most civilised man. Mordecai, on the other hand is a jealous…'

'Did you know him well?' I interrupted.

'I did for a while. You see, it was his idea to go to India to build a hospital there. Mordecai, he wasn't my husband then, decided to go with him. They were both interested in plants and wanted to find out what kinds the Indian people used in their medicines. But it seems the two doctors disagreed over many things and after a year they returned home. Shortly afterwards we married. Their friendship was never the same again. You see, my husband is a businessman and always has an eye for making money. That's his real interest. Your father was dedicated to finding cures and helping people, without any thoughts to money at all. So you see, they were very different men. My husband saw great business opportunities with the East India Company, and while in India he set up all kinds of deals, particularly with opium growers. They keep him supplied today with Indian opium that he uses to make a pain-killing drug called laudanum. My husband is very rich from his factories making mixtures that people pay a lot of money for, in the hope of making them better.'

She sighed sadly so I butted in. 'But isn't that a good thing? It must be good that his medicines are making people better.'

Edith frowned, 'You don't know my father. He lies.'

'The trouble is,' her mother went on, 'my husband sells his medicine for a lot of money to sick people who are so desperate they'll pay anything for a cure. Your father thought this was very wrong and accused him of getting rich on lies and false hopes. When Mordecai announced his Brimstone's Compound cured smallpox, the two men had a terrible row. Your father accused him of curing nothing. You see, much of Brimstone's Compound is no more than coloured rosewater. He sells a stronger mixture for a guinea, which your father said just made people addicted to opium, making them buy even more. If patients get better, my husband takes all the credit but if they die he says they didn't take enough. Either way he wins and makes a fortune.'

'There's some here,' Edith said, holding up a beautiful blue glass bottle with a printed label.

'You'll be able to read it for yourself soon but I can read it to you now if you like…'

BRIMSTONE'S COMPOUND

FOR CURING THE FOLLOWING DISTEMPERS:
ULCERS OF THE LUNGS, SHORTNESS OF BREATH,
COUGHS, PAINS IN THE STOMACH, SCURVY,
COLIC AND WORMS, IN YOUNG OR OLD.
TAKE 30 OR 40 DROPS IN SUGAR, OR WARM ALE.
THIS SPECIAL BREW ALSO CURES BRUISES, STRAINS,
GREEN WOUNDS, SCALDS OR BURNS, LAMENESS FROM
THE RHEUMATISM, AND KNITS BROKEN BONES.

TO CURE THE EVIL SMALLPOX: DRINK ONE WHOLE
BOTTLE ON THE FIRST DAY THE POX APPEARS AND
ANOTHER EACH DAY THEREAFTER.

PRICE FIVE SHILLINGS EACH BOTTLE

When she'd finished reading all the diseases it was meant to cure, she took the stopper out to let me sniff the mixture. It was similar to Master Groundling's gin.

'Yes, there's gin in it, too,' Mrs Brimstone continued. 'People have risked their lives to get hold of that magic liquid. One woman broke into this very house. She was caught and arrested.'

'What happened to her?' I asked.

'She was transported to Australia for seven years for theft. After that I never saw your father again. I know there was a lot of bitterness between the two doctors, especially about ways of treating smallpox. I am sure I survived smallpox because of your father's medicine from the dragon flower tree in our garden. My husband sprinkled me with rose petals and told me I would die. Sadly, your father caught the deadliest strain of the disease and died very quickly. I want you to know, Cephas, he was a lovely man and he was greatly missed by everyone around him.'

I'd sat enthralled by the sad story she told but I still had to ask her, 'And my mother? Did you know her?'

'Yes, but not well. I was at their wedding,' her voice cracked and I could tell she was crying.

'Such a pretty girl. There again, I used to be in those days. Your parents were fine people, Cephas, and so caring. She could have been a doctor, too – if women were allowed. She was always reading science books. Always smiling. It was such a sadness when she died.'

I sat in perfect silence for many minutes, just absorbing what she'd told me, dabbing my eyes. 'How sad that she never held me in her arms,' I said eventually.

Mrs Brimstone leaned forward. 'Of course she did, my dear. You must have been about two and a half... yes, about eight years ago... when she died. Most mysteriously, so they say.'

More pieces of the jigsaw

— Chapter 3 —

The potting shed was my home for several weeks during the bright, warm days of late spring. It was the perfect place for keeping cool under the shade of cherry trees, out of sight from Doctor Brimstone or Mrs Quilter, and for enjoying the stories of Josiah Brimble each morning before he started work. It was an ideal shelter from early summer showers and from which to explore the gardens and lake after breakfast with Edith, once she'd mastered climbing in and out of her window. Most of all, my shed was a fine classroom for learning to read. I traced letters in trays of soil to practise their shapes, and soon I was making whole words and even sentences. I never stopped memorising word patterns, reading anything I could get my hands on. Whenever she could, Edith escaped from the house with books, to join Josiah and me in the shed so that even he began to recognise the written names of different plants.

Each day I visited the dragon flower tree to think of my father and of how he'd planted it after bringing it all the way back from India. Even though I'd found out something about him, I longed to discover so much more. It disturbed me, too, that there was still so much mystery about my mother. I was at least pleased to know we'd been a happy family for the first two years of my life but there were still questions about the tragic deaths of both my parents. Who had taken me to the workhouse and what about the mystery of my tattoo? I wondered if I'd ever find all the missing pieces to my story.

Out of the blue one morning Josiah came into the shed and told me, 'I can take you over the ridge this evening in the cart.'

'Thank you. I'd like to see the countryside around here.'

'Countryside be blowed,' he laughed. 'I'm taking you to see Nellie Hawksworthy. She's expecting you and is more than delighted, I must say.'

By the time the cart rattled into a valley brimming with flowering hedgerows and apple blossom, the sky was a crimson blaze above the hills.

'Just breathe this in – air's thick with scent,' Josiah inhaled with a gasp of pure pleasure. 'Days like this, it's good to be alive, eh?'

He pulled on the reins and the carthorse clattered to a halt by a thatched lychgate. Josiah clucked with a 'There's a girl,' before turning to me. 'I'll wait here, Cephas. Your father's grave is up by the church on the left.'

I had never even thought about my father's grave so I somewhat nervously walked along the path, uncertain as to how I would feel to be standing so close to him. In fact, I felt strangely reassured to be alone in that warm golden light, with swallows swooping overhead, as I looked down at the letters engraved in the stone. I traced them with my finger and spoke aloud. They were letters I now knew and could read:

DOCTOR CORNELIUS CATCHPOLE.

A wreath of flowers, identical to the one I had seen on my own grave, rested against the headstone. I stood quietly and pondered before gasping aloud as a face appeared from among the graves at the side of the church porch. A small elderly woman with white hair under a blue bonnet and in a long turquoise dress stood smiling at me.

'Cephas Catchpole?'

'Yes, ma'am,' I answered, still startled.

'I'm sorry if I surprised you. I told Josiah I'd meet you here. Let me look at you, dear child…'

She held me by the shoulders and looked into my eyes. 'Yes, those eyes,' she smiled, 'the same special glint… like diamonds. Kind eyes and a warm heart. I haven't seen you since you were three years old, scampering round the garden and chuckling all day long. A lovely little boy. Doctor Catchpole thought the absolute world of you.'

She looked down at the grave. 'I see you brought

some flowers.'

'No,' I said. 'In fact, I didn't know…'

She waved at Josiah who was standing on the path. He gestured back before returning to the cart and moving off. 'I told him you can stay with me for a few days. Would you like that?'

'Thank you, Mrs Hawksworthy. Er…'

'Is something the matter, dear?'

'Can I see my mother's grave before we go?'

She touched my arm and looked up at the swallows skimming the church roof and catching flies in the dying light. 'She's not buried here, love. Her grave is a long way away. I'll tell you all I can before long. In the meantime, you can come with me to my cottage for a bite of supper, how's that? It will be a pleasure to look after you again.'

We walked through the village behind a herd of cows being driven by two small boys. Other children played in the meadows, chasing with dogs or cutting hay with scythes. When we came to a tiny cottage, hidden behind lilac and lupins, we entered the one downstairs room, where she told me I'd be sleeping on a feather mattress. I'd never known such luxury.

'Is this where I lived with my father?' I asked.

'Oh no, I've only been here for a few years. You used to live at the other end of the village in a far bigger house, with rooms for patients and a big garden-hut called a pest-house.'

'Who lives there now? Can I see it?'

'I can tell you're going to be full of questions. I can show you what's left of it tomorrow. The remains are all boarded up. There was a fire soon after your father died, I'm afraid. There was nothing left of his study and his work. All his papers were destroyed.'

She put a cloth on the table before taking plates, cups and pots of jam from a cupboard.

'I'm sure you're hungry. Do you know, I'm so thrilled you're here. Nobody knew what happened to you after your father died. It was all a mystery. There were stories that some distant relative was looking after you somewhere.'

'Someone took me to the workhouse. That's where I grew up. They told me there that my mother died when I was born.'

'I didn't know your mother, though she was a lovely lady by all accounts.' As she poured tea from a china pot, the little woman with a kind smile continued thoughtfully. 'After my husband died, I moved to this village and answered an advertisement to be your father's housekeeper. It was just after your mother… went away.'

'Went away? Where did she go?'

'My dear, this is going to be difficult but it's only right that you know the truth.'

We sat at the table and she reached across to place her hands on mine. 'Your father told me what happened and it was no secret at the time. The gossip died down eventually and very few thought she was guilty.'

'Guilty? What do you mean?'

'Your mother was transported. To Australia. Not that she ever got there. Conditions on those ships are so terrible that many die on the journey. Your father never heard from her and it broke his heart, poor man. He always insisted she was innocent but there was nothing he could do. He put all his energy into his work and looking after you. He was devoted to you, Cephas, and it was always a joy to see him with you…'

Once more I felt tears drip from my cheeks as I thought of my father. But to imagine my mother dying at sea was unbearable. 'What crime had my mother committed?'

'She stole a bottle of something from Doctor Brimstone. They caught her in his room one night but your father insisted she wasn't a thief. He was broken-hearted and was inconsolable at losing her. Disease on those ships kills hundreds every voyage, I believe. Tragically, within a year the poor man had joined her in death. That churchyard saw many graves filled by the smallpox that year. The speckled monster, it's called. It was a very sad time for us all.'

We sat talking long into the night and every little detail she described about my father I savoured. At last, when I fell asleep, I dreamed about the man I scarcely remembered but whom I felt I was already getting to know. But I was horrified to think my mother had been arrested as a thief. Surely she hadn't been so desperate to get hold of Brimstone's Compound that she broke in to steal it? It was as I lay in that small cottage room, a cockerel crowing in the garden just outside the window, that I made a promise to myself and my parents that I would find the truth at all costs. I knew that would involve confronting at least two more people and that it would be far from easy. My journey to complete the jigsaw puzzle wasn't over yet. In fact, little did I know, the puzzle was about to become a puzzle within a puzzle. And there was no telling where that would lead.

Discoveries and revelations

—— *Chapter 4* ——

'I've got some things to show you,' Mrs Hawksworthy told me at breakfast. 'I'm afraid I can't help you with them very much as they require reading and I struggle these days, what with my eyesight as well as being quite limited with the written word.'

She put a cutting from a newspaper on the table. 'Your father had this and it was among a few things he asked me to keep. It's nearly eight years old now.

I'd like you to have it.'

Very carefully, and painfully slowly, I began to read the words in front of me aloud.

DAILY GAZETTE

On Monday last, Isabella Catchpole was brought from New-Prison to be further examined before Justice Burke; whereupon she was committed to transportation for seven years, having been charged and found guilty of stealing one corked pot containing inoculation matter of the smallpox from a Doctor Mordecai Brimstone. Whilst she did most manifestly protest that the said matter was designed for malevolent use by Dr Brimstone and that she was protecting the populace, Justice Burke found in favour of the doctor, she being of no medical knowledge nor social standing. Her husband, one Doctor Cornelius Catchpole, did most loudly assist in her defence and in the fierce accusation of Doctor Brimstone. He was duly bound over to keep the peace.

'Those are difficult words, Cephas. You did well to read them.'

I was more concerned with what the words meant. Why did my mother try to steal a pot containing 'matter of the smallpox'? Whatever did that mean? I was both perplexed and saddened, but determined to find out more.

Mrs Hawksworthy reached under the table and picked up a small battered box. 'Your father was a one for keeping scraps of paper. I used to tell him off for leaving pages all over the house! He sent me this box just before he died. It's very dusty, I'm afraid. It's been in my attic and the mice have nibbled the corners.'

'What do you mean when you say he sent it to you? I thought you lived at his house as his housekeeper.'

'I did until he became ill. Both you and I had to leave the house in a hurry. You were taken to another village, I think. Smallpox is so infectious, you see. Doctor Brimstone sent someone to guard the house. Nothing was allowed in and nothing allowed out. Your poor father spent his last days in total isolation. This box was the only thing they let him send out of the house. But I'm afraid there's nothing much in here. At least I'm pleased I can pass it on to you as he'd wished.'

She pushed the box across the table to me. It was tied with string and smeared with dust. I untied the box very carefully, as if it contained a fragile collection of the rarest eggshells. Then I lifted out a small bundle rolled in string. What I found most exciting was a scrap of paper with my father's own handwriting on it – and what's more, it was written to me. I was thrilled to see the words, scrawled in a shaky hand, but nonetheless a direct message from my father. I trembled as I tried to decipher the words, which seemed to make little sense, even after many attempts to read them aloud.

For Cephas,

A record of some of my work and a warning of what might befall you, should we fail to conquer the darkness of our times. Seek the hidden truth within the Family Bible, coded should it fall into the wrong hands.

My life's work has been the eradication of smallpox. Sadly, this is no longer to happen in my lifetime – but I hope it will in yours.

May you grow strong, live well and leave your light to shine hereafter.

Your loving father, Cornelius Catchpole

I re-read his note to me many times but it raised more questions than answers.

'What do you think he means about the Family Bible?'

Mrs Hawksworthy thought for a while. 'Your father certainly did have a large Bible on his desk. I think it was one of the few things they saved from the fire. If I'm not mistaken, it might have gone to the church. They keep old family Bibles in the pews where their owners used to sit.'

'Can I go inside the church and have a look for it?'

'Of course,' she said. 'After all, it's your property now. You should have it.'

We walked through the village towards the place where I was born and lived until I was three. On the way, we stopped at the church. Once more we walked up the path, past my father's grave and into the porch. Mrs Hawksworthy led me inside the dark musty nave, whose smell I vaguely remembered. I searched along the pews and just a few rows back from the pulpit I found a large black Bible with the name Catchpole written on the inside cover. I sat with it in my lap, feeling another special link to my father. I smelt the pages and caressed them, imagining my father reading the words right there each Sunday. The thin pages crackled as I flicked through them, amazed at the millions of tiny words flashing past my eyes. At first, I thought a page had fallen out and fluttered to the floor but when I reached down to pick it up, I saw it was a scrap of paper covered in letters I did not recognise. Was this another language or did I still have many more letters to learn? It looked as if there was a name at the bottom: *Χορνελιυσ Χατχηπολε* – but it meant nothing at all to me. I folded the paper, put it in my pocket and we left the church to find my parents' old home.

I stood looking up at a red-bricked shell of a house, with boards nailed over the door and windows. Brambles and ivy were creeping up the walls, and the roof had many tiles missing. Bricks and timbers were blackened, the chimneys charred and crumbling. I stared for a long time, feeling the strangest sensation. It was as if I knew this place. There was something deep inside me that told me I belonged here. I blinked through wet eyes at the wilderness of a garden that had once presumably been my playground. I imagined my mother and father walking hand in hand around the now overgrown lawns… with me running behind.

'What caused the fire?' I asked.

'It was a mysterious stranger who came one night and set the empty house alight. No one knows who or why but apparently he's still in prison for doing it.'

Seven years of wind, rain, snow and ivy had also left their mark on a wooden hut behind the house. The wood was rotting and many planks were loose.

'That was like a little hospital where people used to recover after being inoculated against smallpox. That meant having smallpox matter rubbed into a cut in the arm. Some patients got very ill, I believe, but both your parents nursed them. If the patients recovered, they'd always be protected from the speckled monster. Your parents stopped their work when you were born so as not to pass the disease to you. Your father inoculated me soon after I came to work here. I was ill for a few weeks but I got over it.'

I hacked my way through nettles to have a closer look and try to peer inside. One of the window shutters was hanging off its hinges so I pulled it and was surprised to see a faded notice still pinned inside. It was when I read the last sentence that I gasped audibly. My father was clearly troubled by the doctor living in the grand mansion not far away. I read the notice to Mrs Hawksworthy, who confirmed that my father was always bothered by Doctor Brimstone and his worrying ways.

INOCULATION

Those who are desirous to take infection of the SMALLPOX by inoculation may find themselves accommodated for the purpose free of charge, by applying to Dr Cornelius Catchpole.

Inoculation, also known as variolation, involves scratching the patient's skin and rubbing powdered smallpox scabs or fluid from pustules into the lesions. In many cases, this practice is known to prevent the severest smallpox occurring in the patient thereafter.

This Pest-House provides accommodation for the period after inoculation, when isolation and nursing will be required for at least two weeks. This treatment is not without risk and can be fatal. It is not for children under the age of five years or the frail.

If you require treatment of the SMALLPOX fever, seek assistance immediately (any time) for free remedies from my pharmacy. These are not cures of the disease but may ease some symptoms.

DO NOT purchase Brimstone's Compound, which is both costly and most non-effectual.

Cornelius Catchpole

I peeled off the notice to take away with me, to show Edith.

'But I'm still confused,' I had to admit. 'If my father inoculated people against smallpox, he must have been inoculated against the disease himself.'

'Of course. All doctors need to be.'

'So why was it that my father caught the disease and died from it?'

'They all said it was from "the black pox" which is even worse. But don't ask me, dear. You really need to talk to a doctor.'

'Yes, I intend to do just that,' I said. 'There's someone who'll be able to tell me, I'm sure. Someone I need to go and see next. But that will mean a journey back into town after dark...'

Meeting the doctor

—— Chapter 5 ——

nce more I skulked in shifting shadows cast by the moon. But I no longer felt like timid prey scuttling from one dark corner to another to escape a predator's eye. Now I was becoming the hunter. The last days of discovery had given me confidence like never before, for I'd become driven with renewed purpose – and the spirit of my father spurred me on. I was hunting the truth and nothing could stop me now. Even so, I still had to keep hidden. Like all hunters, my success would depend on my skills of cunning and surprise. So I crouched in the moonlight among scurrying rats, in the stinking walled yard of the town hospital. And I waited.

The filth and bustle of the streets nearby seemed another world from the peaceful village I'd left that morning. I'd gone back to Brimstone House in Josiah's cart, met Edith to tell her all I'd discovered, leaving her the box of papers, then sneaked once more onto the back of her father's carriage to ride to Gryme Street Hospital. It was there I waited by its back door in all the stinking filth, to seek out someone I felt certain belonged to the shadows.

I looked up at the sound of boots on stone steps. I could just see enough to know this was who I'd come to find. With a silver-topped cane that flashed the moon, in flapping cape and large brimmed hat that covered his face in shadow, the figure descended the steps, brushed past the crate behind which I was hiding, and entered an alley running down to the canal. I emerged from my hiding place, crossed the yard and followed some distance behind.

Hearing boots clumping over the wooden footbridge ahead, I ran to keep close, peering through the mist that rose in reeking swirls from the stinking soup of the sewer below. Holding my breath, I ran stealthily over the bridge to glimpse the hat and flowing cape disappear into a passageway before the mist closed behind. I was frightened now, for in this grey smoky light and the darkest of alleys where no moonlight could reach, villains of the night sought their prey. This was the world of daggers glinting their silver steel in silent flashes every night, as bloodcurdling screams echoed and died, unheard by unconcerned ears.

The figure moved quickly down passages and moonless backstreets, as I hurried to catch up, while keeping my distance so as not to give myself away. As I turned a corner, I stifled a squeal as hands suddenly clasped round my ankles. A drunken beggar, rolling over the cobbles as he pleaded for coins, seized me so tightly that I stumbled and kicked for all I was worth. He swore and groaned before releasing his grip and I ran, tumbling down a black tunnel that cut beneath the canal. It was so dark here that I could see nothing apart from a smudge of light at the far end, where I caught a fleeting silhouette of the hat and cape. So I ran on towards the light and emerged into a deserted street outside the familiar gates of the prison yard. It was eerily quiet here and, apart from two scrawny cats crouching and hissing at each other, nothing stirred. I followed the huge prison wall as it curved away into ever deeper darkness, just as I heard the clang of a gate somewhere ahead. Footsteps crunched away over stones so I ran on, reaching the narrow gate that led into a walled passage at the back of the prison. Very slowly, with the rusty squeak of hinges, I opened the gate and followed the crunching footsteps down a warren of narrow passages between gloomy tenements. In a dribble of light from a porch lamp, I saw damp footprints smeared on steps leading up to a door that clicked shut in front of me. Leaving my own footprints on the stone, I, too, climbed the steps and reached up to the door handle. The heavy door pushed inwards into a hallway, lit by a lantern hanging from a warped, dripping ceiling. Creeping along the hall's sagging floorboards, I listened for the slightest sound in the deathly silence. I turned into a corridor to be faced by a row of peeling doors… but only one had a wet footprint outside. At last I'd pursued my quarry to its lair.

Taking a deep breath and swallowing hard, I stepped forward and tapped on the door. Nothing moved in the hollow silence. I waited, aware only of the pounding heart in my chest. I reached out and knocked again, three sharp taps that echoed around the corridor. As soon as my knuckles struck on the third knock, the door opened a tiny crack, rattling on a chain as a voice hissed, 'Go away,' before the door clicked shut again. Once more I tapped gently but nothing happened, so I bent down, placed my lips to the keyhole and whispered, 'Sitala'.

The door creaked open, revealing eyes shining out of the darkness. A hoarse whisper came back at me like a delayed echo. 'Sitala?'

'Yes,' I said nervously. 'Sitala Mata.'

The chain rattled again, the door opened further and a finger of light brushed across the face in front of me. With a white smile, a flash of the eyes and an urgent, 'Come in, quick,' I was inside.

'Who knows you are here?' a voice asked from the darkness.

'No one,' I answered.

'Are you sure no one followed you?'

'I'm certain.'

'That is good.'

Only then, as he lit a candle, and with the door firmly shut behind us, did the room light up to reveal a cramped space occupied by a bed and a chair. On a table lay the cape and hat I'd been chasing for the last half an hour. Two hands grasped my own and the voice, slow, deep and rich with foreign mystery, spoke my name. 'How did you find me, Cephas?'

'I followed you from the hospital, Doctor, er...'

'Please call me Taggi. I am so delighted you are alive and well. I couldn't believe it was you I glimpsed at the hospital the other night. It was Sitala on your wrist that told me. Let me see her again...But you ran away from me. Why?'

'I was frightened. But now I've got so much I want to ask you about my father.'

'Yes, your father. The wonderful Cornelius. The best friend I ever had. Come and sit on this chair. I shall warm some milk for us and we must talk. I want to know all about you.'

'I've come to find out about you!' I said. 'You're the man of mystery and darkness who knows so many secrets.'

'It is not my choice that I live like this,' he answered.

'But first you must tell me what you already know about me. Then I will tell you what I know. I always wondered what became of you, Cephas. It is so good to see you grown up like this. I always feared the worst.'

I watched this tall, elegant man pour a jug of milk into a pan, then set light to sticks in a fireplace. 'All I know is,' I began, 'you met my father when he went to India and for some reason you came back with him to this country. You are a doctor and you have a secret.'

'I have many,' he grinned, 'but not out of choice.' The sticks were now crackling as flames licked around them and curled up the chimney. He balanced the pan on top and soon a milky steam began to rise.

'You are right,' he went on, 'your father came to my village in India. I was lucky that my father was rich enough for me to learn to read, as well as know some English. Your father taught me so much more and encouraged me to become a doctor. Eventually I came with him here to learn. I lived with him for a while, until he married Isabella.'

'You knew my mother?' I asked eagerly.

'Of course. The lovely Isabella. We were all such

good friends. Your parents helped the sick while I learned medicine and worked in their little hospital. Of course, Doctor Brimstone didn't like it but we didn't care. I came to the city here to learn more in the hospital – not long before you were born. Everything was good until the smallpox epidemic. We tried to inoculate as many people as we could but Doctor Brimstone insisted his medicine would cure them instead. He told us he would infect people to prove he could then cure them. He had a pot of smallpox matter that he intended to scatter in baker's flour to see what happened when people ate the bread. Your parents and I were horrified - think of all the children who could die. We tried to find his pot of smallpox that he planned to release. One night we broke into his study but as we escaped, Isabella got caught. Despite your father and me doing all we could to get her released, no one believed us and the judge declared her guilty of burglary and sent her to Australia where she sadly perished on the journey. Cornelius and I were devastated. It was a terrible time. We carried on treating people who had smallpox but we were now sure Brimstone was infecting them just so they would pay high prices for his mixture. Even his wife caught it and was a victim to his cruel ways. Luckily, I gave her medicine from the dragon flower tree. Cornelius was worried that you, too, would catch "the speckled monster" as he called it – as you were too young to be inoculated. He asked me to take you across the country to a doctor friend who injects babies and children with cowpox...'

'Cowpox? What's that?'

'It's like very weak and harmless smallpox that's just a small rash that you can catch from cows. But if you've had cowpox, you can't catch smallpox. So that's what we did to you. You were vaccinated. The word *vacca* means cow . We marked children who were vaccinated to check they never caught smallpox. And they never did. Many doctors don't believe in vaccination so we set out to prove it works. You were part of the experiment – and as proof you got my tattoo. You and I stayed with the 'cow doctor' as they called him for a few weeks while I helped him and gave tattoos to all the children we vaccinated. They show Sitala, the Indian goddess of smallpox. She is said to protect against the disease. Normally she sits on a donkey but I put her on a cow – *vacca*! So you see, your tattoo means you were protected from smallpox by a cow when you were about three years old. If you look carefully you can see that yours has a little C on each of her feet for Cephas Catchpole. That's how I recognised you.'

I sat mesmerised by his story and looked down at my tattoo with a smile. For the first time, I knew who 'My Lady' was and how she got there. But I still had a burning question. 'Why did Doctor Brimstone have a stone jar with Sitala on it?'

'Ah, yes,' Taggi said, his eyes lighting up. 'I engraved that jar of cowpox vaccine and took it to Brimstone in the hope I could persuade him to vaccinate people instead of sell them his useless mixture. Of course, he laughed at me and said it was just superstitious nonsense. Injecting people with cowpox, he said, would turn them into cows and make them sprout horns and udders. He took the jar and hid it somewhere. I carved Sitala on his dragon flower tree to remind him to treat his poor wife with its soothing properties – as by then she was very ill. But it was then I did a terrible thing for which I beg you to forgive me…'

He looked away from me, seeming very agitated and close to tears. He went to the table to rinse our empty cups in a bowl. 'I was very worried about your father. He was sick and needed to tell me something. I asked Mrs Quilter to look after you at Brimstone House while I returned to look after your father. When I got there, men at his door stopped anyone from seeing him. They said he was highly infectious. They wouldn't even let him send me a written message.'

Taggi sat back on the bed and put his hands to his face. 'I never saw Cornelius again. He died very quickly.'

'From smallpox?' I asked.

'So Brimstone said. The worst kind, called *purpura variolosa*. No one recovers from it.'

'Even if he'd been inoculated against smallpox?' I asked.

'That's just what I questioned. That's why I went back to your father's house after he died. I was sure his notes in his study would give me a clue as to what had been worrying him. So I broke into the house. I was going through his desk when someone smashed the window and threw in a blazing torch. Flames took hold immediately, the door burst open and men grabbed me. I was arrested for setting fire to the house. No one would listen to me. In court my English was not too good and I was found guilty of arson, however much I protested my innocence. They sent me to prison, never to be let out again. I was fortunate not to be executed.'

'So I suppose,' I whispered, 'that's where your secret starts.'

'I was in prison for six years and it was miserable. Brimstone even came there to try out his diseases and medicines on prisoners. Those who agreed to cooperate with him were promised liberation. Very few recovered so it was false hope for them. He just wanted their bodies to dissect in his lectures, where he would charge students to watch his gruesome performances. I spent all my time nursing sick prisoners and using the pus from those sick with smallpox to inoculate the healthy ones to stop the disease spreading through the whole prison. Eventually they saw that I was doing a better job than Brimstone so they told me I could be released on one condition…'

I reached into my pocket and pulled out the pendant I'd found under the gallows.

'I know what you're going to say,' I said as I held up the chain, letting the gold spin one way and then the other, flashing the face of Sitala as it rotated in the candlelight. 'What you might call…'

I smiled as the pendant finally unwound, '…the twist of the hangman.'

'How did you know?' he asked, clearly astonished.

'I was in the crowd on the day you hanged a highwayman. I saw the pendant fall from your neck but I saw something else, too. You stumbled on the steps from the platform and caught your gown…' I looked over to where the very same gown and hood were hooked on the back of the door. 'I caught a quick glimpse of your boots with those special pouches. I've never seen boots like that anywhere else. And as you tugged the gown back into place, I saw the dark skin of your arm. So, as I'd seen you in the hospital shortly before, I knew it must have been you. After all, Indian gentlemen in boots like that are very rare round here!'

'You are the only one who knows. I never want anyone else to know that I am Titus the Rope. I hate doing the job but if I didn't do it, they wouldn't let me out to work in the hospital at nights. That is the agreement and the work I need to do. You see, just like your parents, I believe I must work hard at fighting diseases and suffering. It can be dangerous and heart-breaking but, just like the doctor with the cowpox, there can be great breakthroughs.

Occasionally, there are one or two doctors who are more concerned with gaining money and power. They are the ones, like Brimstone, who make things worse for all of us. That is why we must fight back, just like Isabella and Cornelius did so bravely. This dismal room belongs to the prison but I can come and go so long as I register each morning and evening. In one more year, if I do my duty as hangman and break no rules, I shall be free.'

I couldn't believe that this gentlest of men had to live like this. 'We've all been imprisoned in some way or other because of Doctor Brimstone,' I said angrily.

'He is a powerful man who has to be in control of others,' Taggi said. 'And he is an evil man who must be stopped. My dream is to see him brought to justice before I return to India.'

'You want to go home?'

'More than anything in the world. Wouldn't you, rather than live like this? I am trying to save money for my passage back to India where I need to tend the sick. I just don't belong here any more. At least back home I can be who I really am, without needing to hide under a hood or only daring to go out after dark. But enough of me, Cephas. What happened to you after I left you with Mrs Quilter all those years ago?'

'I ended up at the workhouse. That was a terrible place. It wasn't much better being a chimney sweep. Then I ended up buried in a coffin. But things got better at last! I'm astounded to find out about my parents. I've cried a lot for them, but I'm really proud of them and I feel that I'm getting to know them at last.'

'They were truly beautiful people. And you, Cephas, have many of their fine ways. But who is looking after you now?'

'Sitala,' I smiled. 'Can I stay here tonight?'

'You are welcome. It won't be the first time I have looked after you. You seem a wise boy, Cephas. I know your father would be most proud of you. But you know, I think he sensed many of the things that were to happen before they did. Sadly, he was unable to change many of them for the better.'

'Then it will be up to me to take over where he left off,' I announced proudly. 'I've just made up my mind to follow in his footsteps. That will mean confronting the dreaded Doctor Brimstone face to face – just like he did. I know it will be dangerous so I'm going to think of a plan before taking the biggest risk of my life.'

To hospital

─── *Chapter 6* ───

The morning mist crept up from the drains, prowled the streets and stalked through the runnels and tunnels around the slimy prison walls. My footsteps echoed through a maze of passages as I emerged, unseen, from Taggi's dismal quarters. A long walk lay ahead of me, all the way to Brimstone House where I hoped to make sense of the thousand thoughts churning in my head. I'd learned so much in the last few hours that I needed the day's walk to sort my mind and finalise my plan.

Dodging between lumbering horse-drawn wagons and traders setting out their stalls, I strode on through the streets, past the usual groups of children huddled in doorways or sprawled beneath bridges. It was as I turned down a passageway between taverns that a hand grabbed my shoulder and pulled me down a flight of steps to a cellar. I fell to my knees and squinted up at the man now gripping me by the collar.

'Good mornin', Angel, my boy. And what brings you to these parts?'

I stammered awkwardly, not knowing what to say. 'Er… good day, Mr Cutpurse. How are you?' Jack Cutpurse was none other than the graverobber and thief from whom I'd escaped.

'All the better for seein' you, old friend. What a shame you left without leaving details of your new residence. Plenty of nice hot baths, I trust? You appear to be of more radiant countenance than I recall.' He cackled and let go of my collar.

'I'm sorry I didn't say goodbye,' I said, getting to my feet and brushing myself down, 'but I had to visit someone and find some information.'

'Did yer now? I 'ope it wasn't h'information what

you gave away.'

'No, honest… I've told no one about you, really. No information at all.'

'Very wise of you, Angel. It's funny you should mention h'imformation, as it's h'imformation I have for you, my boy. H'imformation concerning Tooth, my young nephew, you may recall.'

'How's he getting on?'

'Not good. Not good. H'infact, you might say things are very bad indeed.'

'I'm sorry to hear that.'

'Listen, I didn't mean to manhandle you too roughly just now. It's just that it was a surprise to see you in broad daylight and I didn't want to lose you for a second time. Seein' as yer a bit of an h'expert at slippin' away. Look, why don't we go somewhere more pleasant where we can talk, eh?' Jack climbed back up the steps, looked up and down the passage and beckoned me to follow. He led me into a back room of a tavern where a few men played cards on benches in a smoky haze. There were tankards of ale on a table and a greyhound stretched under it, dribbling in the sawdust.

'We'll sit in that corner there,' Jack pointed, 'I'll

get us something to cheer our hearts. Don't look so scared, my boy. I'm not goin' to harm yer.'

He brought two drinks to our gloomy corner but I could only bear to take the smallest of sips. 'I'm afraid to say,' he began, 'that Tooth is not a well boy. He's been taken to the isolation hospital on account of the pox fever. Being summer, he's been living out on the streets and it seems he picked up the disease from them he befriended. I'm not allowed anywhere near him, of course – so the poor lad must be suffering alone somewhat. Mind you, they took in his cousin Lotty as well only this mornin'. So at least he'll know someone.'

'Both of them have got smallpox?'

'She's been sleepin' where he slept one night so I reckon she caught it from the bedding.'

'My father used to look after people with smallpox,' I said proudly. It was the first time I'd announced the fact and, although it made me feel immensely important to say it, Jack didn't seem very impressed.

'Did he now? The thing is, Tooth is my own nephew and I am of an anxious state of mind.'

'It must be a worry,' I said, forcing one more sip of the horrible brew in my tankard. I spluttered,

'I just hope they don't give him any of that Brimstone's Compound.'

It was as if I'd just cursed the vilest oath, for Jack choked and turned on me angrily. 'Don't mention that man. He's nothing but a cheat and criminal.' Had he not sounded so angry, I would have dared to suggest that it was a bit rich for Jack, of all people, to accuse someone else of being a criminal. He leaned forward and whispered, 'We'd supplied that Brimstone with bodies what he paid for, but then he asks us to collect from the docks a "few supplies" as he calls it. Some sort of smugglin' and he wanted us to do the dirty work of takin' all the risks. So Horace and me go down the docks and collect the barrels off a ship and get 'em to his room at the 'ospital. But instead of payin' us as agreed, he starts the blackmail. If we don't collect the same each week, he'll go to the authorities about our night-time activities. I ask yer, how dishonest is that?'

I stifled a smile and asked him what they were going to do about it.

'Horace is all for getting violent,' he went on. 'But that could get us in deep trouble.'

'The reason I escaped from your house was

because Horace talked of murdering people,'
I told him.

'I thought as much. Fear not, my dear, we've
never killed a soul. After you left, we thought you'd
shop us all so we changed our plans, so to speak.
To be honest, which I can be at times,' he chuckled
into his tankard, 'you did me a favour, Angel. I was
never keen on what Horace was scheming. I talked
him out of it but now I'm all for breaking into
Brimstone's room to steal back what we delivered.
That would teach him to pay up for our services or
he don't get the goods he wants.'

'That would seem the best way,' I said. 'From
what I've learned about Doctor Brimstone, he
hates it if he doesn't get his own way.'

'Quite right. That's why I gave Tooth the job
of getting me the key to Brimstone's room at the
hospital. Tooth said it'd be simple to sneak in the
window, lift the key off the hook and get it to me.
The trouble is, he can't get it to me on account that
both Tooth and the key are currently locked away
inside that isolation hospital.'

Whether it was the effect of what I'd been sipping,
or whether it was just a moment of total madness,
I suddenly had an outrageous idea. Knowing that

Jack and Horace were seeking revenge against Doctor Brimstone could be very useful to my plan. 'I could get you the key,' I blurted. 'If you promise to help me.'

'Angel, my lad, though it's most kind of you to offer, you'd have to find Tooth and risk the pox. You might be an angel with the protecting hands of the Almighty about yer, but you could catch yer death.'

'No I wouldn't,' I grinned. 'We angels don't catch smallpox. Sitala's already made sure of that!'

Jack looked around furtively and whispered in my ear. 'So what are you saying, exactly?'

I told him, 'If I get you that key, will you and Horace help me when I have to face Doctor Brimstone? All I'll want you to do is deliver him a sack with something unusual in it. What do you think, Jack?'

He shook me by the hand after looking behind him again. 'It's a pleasure doing business with you, my dear. I'll be most grateful for your help. So would Horace. In fact, you'll be delighted to know that his missus said you were a fine lad after all. That hangman's rope you got her helped her neck ailment a treat, you see. And if she's 'appy, we're all 'appy.'

'Maybe I've just got healing hands. We angels do have them sometimes, you know. It must run in my family.'

'Then I hope you can do the same for Tooth soon. When can you get in to see him?'

'How about right now?'

'Really?'

'On one condition,' I said.

'What's that, Angel?'

I passed him my tankard. 'So long as I don't have to drink any more of this.'

The isolation hospital was an imposing building of three storeys, topped with a clock tower and fronted by high iron gates. It stood proudly between warehouses and merchants' quarters by the canal, which shone under a blue sky and blazing sunshine.

'Tooth could be anywhere in that lot,' Jack said as we stood outside the gates. 'Poor boy must feel like he's in a sweltering prison. Give him these, will yer?'

He squeezed two cold sausages into my hand so I smiled, stuffed them in my pocket and scaled the gates. I told Jack I would see him later and was soon standing at the steps of the pillared main entrance, wondering how I was going to get inside. There were bars over all the ground floor windows but, being such a warm day, many windows were open upstairs. I chose a first-floor window round the back, just above the flat roof of a porch. There were enough grooves between the stone blocks of the walls for me to get foot and hand holds, so I was soon up on the porch roof and slithering inside the open window above.

I found myself in a long corridor, full of unpleasant smells, moans and wails. Many open doorways led from it into rooms crammed with beds or straw mattresses, occupied by the most pathetic specimens of humanity. Patients wandered around aimlessly, whilst others lay motionless or sat groaning. Some were partly dressed, some in dishevelled gowns, others naked. No one took the slightest notice of me but then I saw a formidable woman striding around demanding that everyone go to sleep. Many patients were covered in rashes or blisters, with scaly sores and weeping pustules. I must have looked pale in comparison to the burning faces around me – so I turned a corner where no one could see me and I slapped my face hard, many times. My eyes were streaming and my cheeks were numb and sweating. Suddenly I was aware of the woman in charge staring at me. 'Why are you out of your bed?'

'I just want some air, it's so hot.'

'Then go and sit by a window, you look terrible.'

'I've lost my way. I'm not sure where I am. My bed was near the boy called Tooth Cutpurse.'

'Then you've certainly wandered far, you turnip head. It's up those stairs and second on the right. Hurry up now and get to sleep. I don't want to see you on the prowl again.'

I walked back along the corridor, peering in the wards as I passed. Each one looked more desperate than the one before. All patients were mixed together: children, babies, men, women and the elderly, some tied together or strapped in their beds, others sprawled on sacks on the floor. Some appeared exactly as if they had been severely scalded or burned, with one old lady shrieking that she was on fire. She and others reeked of a peculiarly sickening odour so I passed quickly on to the stone stairs.

I dreaded what I might see in Tooth's ward and whether I'd even recognise him. I walked through the doorway, just avoiding someone being sick into a bucket and as I looked up I heard a whistle followed by a 'Cor love us, look who it ain't! Angel, me old turnip!'

Tooth was sitting up, grinning characteristically, but his face was a mass of scabby blisters. He winked at me and whispered, 'What are yer doin' 'ere – don't yer know it's catching?'

I smiled at him and shook him by the hand. 'You're forgetting I'm an angel! How are you, Tooth?'

'Bored. There's nothin' to do and nothing to thieve – apart from a bit more of the dreadful broth they feed yer. They tell us it sweetens the blood and we ain't allowed solid food. I'm dying for a pig puddin'.'

'Then you might like these from Uncle Jack.' I held out the squashed sausages, which he snatched with delight before adding secretly, 'Have you seen my cousin, Spotty Lotty? That's her being sick by the door. Poor girl is rough as a hedgehog's buttocks. I was like that to begin with. But I don't feel so bad now – not like some in 'ere. Oi, Lotty, look who's 'ere.'

She looked up and tried to smile, gave a feeble wave and hurriedly returned to her bucket. The man next to Tooth swore and told him to keep quiet, just as a baby in a basket began squawking like a strangled parrot.

'Jack asked me to get the key from you,' I whispered. 'The one to Brimstone's room.'

'It will be my pleasure, squire,' he winked and he reached into his sock. 'I'd forgot it was there. Come to think of it, I wondered why I'd been walkin' funny!' He handed it to me and I pushed it into my pocket, just as the baby started to choke in distressing convulsions. Tooth rushed over, picked the baby up and tried to comfort it but the cries worsened, causing many of the other patients to start cursing. The poor child's face was covered in a scarlet crust, with a neck like an angry lizard's. A doctor in a bloodied apron strode into the room and took charge. 'Give me that baby and you get into bed. Everybody get to sleep. And what are you doing in here, boy?'

He was waving a finger at me aggressively. 'This is not your room so just get back to where you belong. You'll be punished if I see you again.'

I waved to Tooth and Lotty before running out, down the stairs and along the corridor to the window I'd climbed through. Within minutes I was back outside in scorching sunshine and walking down the drive towards the gates where Jack still sat waiting, dozing in the heat.

'One key,' I said, pressing it against his cheek. He snuffled and snorted as he woke.

'God bless you, my child. You are nothing short of an absolute angelic genius.'

'I'm pleased to be of service, sir,' I bowed and pretended to doff my cap. 'And I trust you may now be prepared to assist me in my plan.'

'Anything you say, Angel,' he said. 'But prey, do tell… what exactly is it you want us to do?'

'It's perfectly simple,' I smiled. 'You just have to deliver Doctor Brimstone another body in a sack.'

'It's a waste of time, he won't pay yer for it.'

'He doesn't have to. That's because I'll want it back.'

He looked at me as if I was completely mad. 'You want to keep a dead body?'

'Who said it would be dead?' I asked with a wink. 'In fact, I hope it will be very much alive. You see, the body in the sack that I want you to deliver will be none other than myself.'

The hidden message

—— *Chapter 7* ——

Rage bubbled inside me and spilled out with huge force. Edith tried to calm me but I'd never felt so angry before. Seeing her again seemed to release all the hatred for her father I'd been holding back. I clenched my fists and pounded her pillow. 'Your father has ruined my life! He destroyed my mother by getting her sent away and he got Taggi thrown in prison. Taggi is a lovely man and he'd have looked after me – but I ended up at that wretched workhouse because of your father. I hate him.'

Edith held me, 'And I hate him, too. We all do. I'm so sorry he did all that to you, Cephas. But now we can fight him together.'

Tears were streaming down both our faces. 'My mother broke into this house to steal the smallpox that your father was using to infect people. They caught her and she was sent to Australia where she...' I couldn't continue. I was so racked with sobs I could hardly breathe. Edith stroked my cheek and waited for me to calm down. Eventually, with runny nose and dribbling mouth, I took a big sniff and spluttered, 'My father might still be alive today if it wasn't for all the worry that weakened him so much. In the end, he was destroyed by the very disease he'd been fighting for so long...'

When I regained control, I remembered what I'd been meaning to do. It was to check again the letter my father had left for me and I needed Edith to help. I hadn't even examined the scrap of paper I'd found in the Bible. What did all those strange letters mean? I fumbled in my pocket for the note. I saw the shaky writing at the top and knew this was one of the last things my father ever wrote.

'What do you think this weird writing means?' I asked.

Edith looked closely at every mark on the paper. 'It looks like Greek letters. I can't read Greek. It must be something biblical.'

I dried my eyes and wiped my nose while she pondered, drumming her fingers on the table. 'The last two words look like they could be a name – with the same number of letters as your father's. What if your father simply replaced each letter in his message with a Greek symbol? If *Χορνελιυσ Χατχηπολε* says Cornelius Catchpole, I might be able to work out where the same letters of his name appear in the rest of the message. Then I might make words through the process of elimination, deduction or complete guesswork!'

Edith studied each letter in the name then began to replace letters in the message with English letters if they matched. It took her a long time to decipher it while I just stared at the code – it was just like being unable to read again.

Ι αμ στρυγγλιυγ το σταψ χονσχιουσ βυτ τηισ ισ νοτ σμαλλποξ Ι αμ δψιυγ φρομ. Ι ηατⲱε βεεν ποισονεδ βψ α λετηαλ συβστανχε χρεατεδ βψ Μορδεχαι Βριμστονε. Ηε ηασ φιναλλψ κιλλεδ με φυστ ασ Ι ωασ αβουτ το εξποσε ηιμ φορ κιλλιυγ μανψ. Ηε μυστ βε στοππεδ φρομ ηισ ετιλ χριμεσ ανδ βρουγητ το φυστιχε βεφορε μορε ποορ σουλσ αρε μαδε το συφφερ ατ τηε ηανδσ οφ τηισ χρυελ μυρδερερ.

Χορνελιυσ Χατχηπολε.

She soon realised *χ* was c, *o* was o, *ρ* was r, *ν* was n, *ε* was e, *λ* was l, *ι* was i, *υ* was u and *σ* was s. And so, together, letter by letter, word by word, we gradually decoded the message. With every sentence we completed, the tension mounted and my anger grew until I finally realised the awful truth of what my father was telling me.

Once more I was reduced to sobs, shaking in my turmoil of grief and fury. Edith, too, sat weeping, unable to speak and kicking at her bed. Such was our total exasperation that we cried long and loud… and were unaware that the bedroom door was quietly being opened.

'Whatever's going on in here?' Mrs Quilter entered the room and stared in disbelief, even though she had yet to see my face for my head was in my hands as I lay on the bed.

'Edith! There's a boy in your room. Whatever will your father say?'

'I don't care,' Edith shouted back. 'Besides, he won't know unless you go running to tell him like you do about everything.'

'Now listen here, young lady…'

'No, you listen to me for a change…' Edith stomped across the room, past Mrs Quilter and stood in front of the door. 'You won't be able to run out when you learn the truth.'

'What truth? What are you saying girl? How dare you speak to me as if…'

'Stop your gabbling, Mrs Quilter,' she interrupted her, 'and see who my friend is.'

Until then I'd been lying face-down. I slowly lifted myself up, turned and faced Mrs Quilter. As soon as she saw my face, she screamed. She turned to run but Edith barred her way.

'I think you know something about my good friend Cephas Catchpole,' Edith said calmly. Mrs Quilter took another look at me and whimpered. 'But he's dead!'

'I've come back,' I croaked. With all my crying, my face must have looked flushed, tear-stained and horrific, for she backed away muttering something about the living dead.

'But I would have been very much alive if it

weren't for you and Doctor Brimstone,' I croaked. She said nothing, but lifted her apron to hide her eyes.

'My father won't be home until late tonight,' Edith said. 'So you won't be able to hold his hand like you normally do. Instead you must think about how cruel you've been.'

'I wasn't cruel,' she howled. 'It was me who took him as a three-year-old to be looked after at Brickdyke workhouse. Doctor Brimstone said that was the best place for him.'

'Even though Doctor Taggi wanted to look after me,' I shouted.

'He couldn't because he went to prison for arson. So, I told them at the workhouse that you were a foundling and needed a good home.'

'And what did you tell them about my parents?' I stepped closer as she continued to cower.

'I said your mother died giving birth to you and your father died of the pox. I didn't want them to know your mother was really a convict. So I did you a favour, see. Otherwise they might have treated you like a convict yourself.'

'They treated us all like wicked convicts. No one ever came to see me. Did no one here ever think to come to visit me over the years? Can you imagine how lonely and miserable my life was? I had no one in the whole world.'

'You had that elderly aunt of your mother's.'

I stood and stared at her, as a cold shiver ran through my whole body. I caught sight of myself in the looking glass and was horrified at my reflection.

'Who?' My voice cracked, gurgling from my throat in a hoarse whisper.

'A grey-haired lady who came to this house a few weeks ago. She said she was your great aunt and lived somewhere by the sea. She'd come looking for your father and you. So I told her you were both dead. She asked where you were buried so I told her and she parted with no further ado. She asked where she could buy two wreaths and that was it. She left.'

'What's her name?' I was still barely able to speak.

'I can't remember. She was a miss someone or other. Miss Harper? Or Miss Harvest… Something like that.'

Edith smiled at me. 'You've got a living relative, after all, Cephas!'

There was a moment's pause while Mrs Quilter eyed me up and down nervously. 'He looks so real,' she stuttered, 'for a ghost. And to think, I helped to put him in that box. I saw him dead with my own eyes. How did he get out and get in here?'

'It's easy,' I said. 'I just pass through solid walls… whooooooer.'

She gave another whimper and pushed past Edith, clawing at the door. She pulled it open and ran, screaming all the way back to the kitchen.

I looked at Edith and smiled. 'That will give her plenty to think about!'

'Yes, but she's bound to tell my father. He'll probably think she's been seeing things but…'

'Then it's important I get to your father before she does,' I said. 'I've got to face him with the truth and catch him off his guard. He's going to pay for what he did to my father. You do see that, don't you?'

'Of course, and my mother will think the same. It's only right that father is made to confess to his crimes and must answer for doing such a wicked thing. But of course, he won't listen to a word you tell him.'

'I know but I've thought of that. With Horace Dalrymple and Jack Cutpurse holding him down, he'll have to listen to what I've got to say. And if I can, I'll get a written confession out of him. I owe it to my parents.'

'Take care, Cephas. My father can turn very nasty, you know. I think I should come with you.'

Much that I wanted Edith to be there, I knew her father would confess nothing in front of her.

'No, Edith, I've faced most of this by myself and I've got to be brave up to the end.'

'Then I insist on coming with you and waiting outside. Josiah can take us in the cart and we'll bring you back here again afterwards. After all, I'll be desperate to know what happens.'

I wiped my face, took a deep breath and touched her hand. 'Thank you.'

We said no more but each of us stared at Edith's translation of my dear father's dying message – disguised in Greek letters and hidden in a Bible to ensure the killer never realised the evidence against him was preserved on a scrap of paper. It was now up to me to confront that killer with the words clasped in my hand.

I am struggling to stay conscious but this is not smallpox I am dying from. I have been poisoned by a lethal substance created by Mordecai Brimstone. He has finally killed me just as I was about to expose him for killing many. He must be stopped from his evil crimes and brought to justice before more poor souls are made to suffer at the hands of this cruel murderer.

Cornelius Catchpole.

The demon doctor

— Chapter 8 —

he cart drew up outside Gryme Street Hospital with a grunt from Josiah at the reins. 'The best of luck to you all.' Jack and Horace climbed down with a sack, while Edith smeared some of her father's white wig-powder over my face. With a little charcoal rubbed under my eyes and a dab of rouge to the eyelids and grass-green to the lips, I looked as deathly as any corpse you could possibly meet. Dressed in a long white shroud, I climbed from the cart and stepped inside the sack.

'We'll wait here for you,' Edith called, as Jack and Horace carried me to the back of the hospital, to the yard outside Brimstone's room.

'I've got the key,' Jack said, 'so we can get inside and be ready for him.'

Horace sounded as aggressive as ever. 'And I'll lock it again once he arrives so he can't get out. I'm going to enjoy this. It's about time we made this one squirm. I've got an iron bar down me breeches and I'll use it if need be.'

'Please, no violence,' I called from the sack. 'I just want him to hear what I've got to say.'

They carried me up the steps and unlocked the door. We went inside to wait in the darkness. I remained inside the sack, stretched out on a large table where countless corpses had lain before. After a short while, the door opened and I lay very still as I heard a candle being lit.

'What the devil are you doing in here?' I knew instantly it was Doctor Brimstone's voice.

'We've brought you a present,' Horace began.

'How did you get in here?'

'With a key that I'm about to use to lock us in. There's no other way out.' I heard the key turn in the lock.

'I could get you transported for this. It's breaking and entering.' Brimstone was clearly agitated and alarmed.

Jack spoke next, almost in a whisper. 'Don't you want to see what's in the sack?'

Brimstone roared, 'I won't pay you a penny.'

'We told you it's a present,' Horace joined in, 'because we like you so much. Have it as a gift. It's in perfect condition and very fresh.'

I felt the sack being tugged and saw the candle through the holes, as it was plonked on the table beside me.

'Allow me to assist,' Jack said, and he pulled me from the sack, face down.

'It's only a child,' Brimstone snapped. 'That's no good. Too skinny by far.'

Jack rolled me over. 'Then look at his face and see what you think.'

There was a long silence as the candle flame was brought, quivering, up to my face. Doctor Brimstone's voice was different now. There was an edge of fear.

'Where did you get this creature? He looks like…' He lifted my hand to look at my wrist.

'By Jove, it's him again… and he's warm!' It

was then I sat bolt upright and opened my eyes. 'Good evening, Doctor Brimstone, do you know who I am?'

The sight of him backing away so fast with a look of such horror in his eyes gave me a surge of confidence and extra daring. 'Lost your tongue, Doctor Brimstone? Try mine…'

I stuck out my tongue and wiggled it at him. He was visibly shaking and his voice trembled. 'How can this be? He's been buried for weeks.'

I fixed him with a stare and spoke again, very slowly as if in a trance. 'But I couldn't just rot in my grave when I had unfinished business to settle.'

'To what business do you refer? This is some sort of sick joke.' He stepped forward, regaining some of his courage but Horace stepped towards him threateningly.

'Do you know who I am?' I asked.

'I have no idea, although you pretend to be the dead chimney sweep. I will not be menaced in my own room.'

I felt the anger rising inside me again. 'You dare to talk about menace after what you did to my mother?'

'I have no idea what you are talking about and if you don't get out of here, I will strike you – dead or not.' He raised his fist.

'You will do no such thing,' Horace growled, taking the iron bar from his belt.

'This is some sort of conspiracy,' Brimstone shouted. 'Just because I've threatened to send you two behind bars for your criminal ways.'

'No,' I said. 'It is me who asked them to come here. As witnesses.'

'Witnesses?'

'Yes, to what I have to say. You killed my father. You are nothing but a murderer.' My rage at his defiance spurred me on and nothing would stop me now.

'Your father? I have no idea who you mean and it's all lies.'

'My father was...' I paused and lifted the candle to his face to watch for a reaction.

'My father was Doctor Cornelius Catchpole.'

The reaction was greater than I'd expected. His nostrils flared, his cheek twitched and his eyes narrowed. 'You're... Cephas Catchpole?' he said softly.

'I am. And you destroyed my parents because they were better doctors than you will ever be. You were so jealous of them that you had to stoop to your evil ways to get fame and fortune, all from the suffering of others. Admit it, Doctor Brimstone…'

For some seconds, he was unable to speak before he croaked, with an ashen face, 'How do you know all this? Who told you?'

'I've made it my business to find out,' I said. 'So, do you confess to your crimes?'

'And what if I do? You've no proof of anything.' He was regaining his bravado once more. So I added, 'My father wrote it all down. I have his papers.'

'Nonsense,' he snapped. 'They were destroyed. The fire got rid of everything.'

'You started the fire to destroy his work. The fire you blamed on Doctor Taggi.'

I kept on, as I took a copy of my father's note from my sleeve, 'It wasn't enough to destroy my father, you destroyed his home, too.'

I slowly read out my father's accusation. Brimstone's face appeared frozen.

It was Jack who spoke next, dangerously soft and menacing. He'd been listening throughout, still and silent. 'I think we have heard enough. Brimstone, you're as guilty as sin. My friend and I are witnesses and it's high time you were brought to justice.'

It was as if Jack's words lit a fuse, for suddenly Doctor Brimstone thawed and screeched at the top of his voice. 'How dare you reprobates come in here to a city hospital run by dedicated doctors to make such accusations. You're nothing but ruffians and no court in the land would ever listen to the mouths of such vermin… whereas I am regarded with the highest renown for miles. I regularly dine with city chiefs and bankers, judges and bishops. I am a man of great wealth and influence. Whoever will believe the accusations you make? You're here to blackmail and ridicule me. So I suggest you leave the premises to which you illegally gained entry and get out of here before I call the constables to have you all apprehended and beaten.'

'Why you, I'll strike you down for this...' Horace lunged forward with the bar above his head.

'No, stop!' I shouted. 'Please don't strike. We've all heard enough. We know the truth and that's why I came. I want you to know, Doctor Brimstone, that I hold you responsible for the deaths of my parents and for sending me to the workhouse and you need to answer for it.'

'Very well,' Doctor Brimstone said in a sudden change of tone and taking paper from his desk. 'I will write my confession and then you can go.'

He dipped his quill into ink and scratched a few lines across the page while we stood watching. He sprinkled blotting sand over his writing before shaking it off, folding the paper twice and handing it to me. 'There, now leave these premises and never return.'

I unfolded the paper. 'I will have to read it first.'

'Don't be absurd,' he laughed, 'you're just a chimney sweep boy from the workhouse. You couldn't read if you tried. You didn't think I really believed you read that made-up twaddle from your father just then. You're no more than an ignorant peasant who pretended to read but just made it all up. You didn't let me see what was written, did you?'

'That was part of my plan,' I smiled, as my eyes sped along the rows of his meaningless scrawl of jumbled letters. 'You can't fool me with this nonsense. I can read perfectly thanks to a very good teacher you may know. And it would seem I am able to read far better than you are able to write. I wonder what your aristocratic friends would make of your rather feeble attempt to fool me with nothing but meaningless scribble – and in not a very legible hand for an educated man.'

Horace and Jack laughed, which clearly filled him with rage. 'Very well,' he hissed, 'State your price. How much must I give you to make you leave?'

I saw the glint in Jack's eye so I replied before they had the chance to name their fee. 'You know very well it isn't money I want. I want you to admit how cruel you've been and to realise you've been found out. Are you sorry for the misery you've caused?'

He froze again, in deep thought, looking nervously at the bar in Horace's hand. 'Very well, I apologise.'

'Say it again,' Horace sneered.

'I apologise.'

I knew it was just a game he was playing but at least I'd shown him I wasn't too scared to face him. I'd made my point and I wanted to get away to plan what to do next. So I warned him the truth would be revealed to all in time.

He swore as we shuffled out laughing, followed by insults hurled at us and Horace mumbling threats that he'd come back and use his iron bar if Doctor Brimstone ever upset us again. We returned to the cart where I removed my shroud and told Edith about the encounter.

'We nearly scared him to death. You were very good, Angel,' Jack said.

'I'm all for giving him another dose,' Horace added as they climbed in the cart. 'But we'll return tomorrow to take back what he owes us. We've still got his key.'

I thanked them for helping me, as I knew I wouldn't have stayed safe without them. But there were still many things on my mind that I needed to sort out so I told Edith I'd see her in a few days. Taggi was expecting me back at his room so I bid them goodnight.

'Are you sure you'll be all right alone on these streets, Angel?' Jack looked genuinely concerned. 'After all, you wouldn't want to end up in the wrong hands, would yer now?'

'I think I'm getting used to looking after myself, thank you,' I said and I waved them off before turning to walk along the alley leading down to the canal.

After the heat of the day, the night was sultry, with a golden haze around the moon. Long before I saw the bridge, I could smell the steamy sewer beneath it and hear the bubbling of its rancid broth. I took a deep breath and hurried across the planks, the rank steam swirling around my feet. I was halfway across when, from nowhere, hands suddenly grabbed my throat, strangled my scream and dragged me to the floor. Sprawling face-down, I choked as my head hung over the side of the planks, staring into the stinking brew below where the reflection of the moon curdled in its steaming slops. The hands gripped my shoulders and flipped me over so that I lay on my back, looking up into the sweating, furious face of Doctor Brimstone. His knee pressed down on my chest and his fingers dug into my neck.

'You thought you were so clever, with your feeble-minded guards to protect you. Well you're not so clever now, walking on your own at night where no one can hear your screams. You're just like your father, thinking you're too smart for me, with your beliefs of right and wrong. And just like your father, you need to be stopped. I've made more money than he ever dreamed of and everyone knows how successful I've been. They all know my name at the College of Surgeons but no one's ever heard of Catchpole, the failure.'

I could hardly breathe let alone speak but I had to splutter what I was thinking. 'You're hardly successful when your own wife and daughter despise you…'

The blow to my face stunned me and I felt the

trickle of blood from a split lip but I had the presence of mind to twist my head and bite the fingers at my throat. He let go with a curse as I sucked in the stinking air that made me retch. He crouched over me, grabbed me by the collar and pulled me up to my feet. Then he slammed me against the rail of the bridge that shook and cracked with the force. I was winded and crumpled, but he dragged me up again, bringing his sweaty nose right up to mine.

'I'll go down in history for my famous medicine. Not like your father with all his talk of cowpox and vaccination rubbish. He was getting too big for himself – just like you are. That's why I'm going to get rid of you the way I got rid of him. He was hoist by his own petard. In other words, his own medicine killed him… with a little help from me, of course.'

He reached into a pocket and brought out a small bottle and held it up to my eyes.

'See this? Cornelius used my land to grow his famous foxgloves. He made digitalis from them. He was sure it cured diseases. But in my hands, it does something else. It's deadly the way I make it. Slip it into a hot drink and within hours the drinker will die. Of course, your father knew that

I'd poisoned him – when it was too late. It took two days for him to expire. That's why I hired men to guard his house to stop his messages getting out. I said he was in isolation because he had smallpox. I knew he'd try to get word out somehow so I burnt the place to get rid of any notes he'd left behind. So, I don't see how he could possibly have written to you. Tell me how he did it. How did you know the truth?'

He was shouting and spitting with fury now and the hate burned in his eyes. Frightened as I was, I replied, 'My father was just too clever for you. As you heard, his last message to me was in code and said that you'd have to confess for your crimes. And as you've just done that, my father wins again!'

Spitting with rage, he took the stopper from the bottle clenched in his hand. 'This is going down your throat and when they find your body in the sewer, you'll be dragged out and buried like any other urchin boy. But this time you won't get out of your grave. And those grave-robber friends of yours won't come to your aid as I'll make it my duty to get them both hanged. Now give me your father's note and I will destroy the evidence.'

He grabbed the paper from my sleeve and ripped

it to shreds before grasping my throat even tighter. As I struggled in a vain attempt to release myself from his grip, he bent my back over the rail of the bridge, pushing me against it with agonising force. I squealed as his right hand clasped my jaw, forcing my mouth open and his other hand poured the bitter poison between my lips. It was as I kicked and spluttered that a deafening crack ripped through the night. The rail snapped and I fell backwards. The splintering wood flew into the air before plopping into the seething sewage below, as I grabbed at one of the posts on the bridge. My legs swung out over the drop but I clung on by my fingertips. Brimstone, having been leaning so heavily on me, tottered forward to the edge, dropped the bottle and staggered to regain his balance. His foot crunched on glass, skidding on spilt poison. With a bloodcurdling scream, he slid past me, brushing against my feet as he plunged with a squelching slosh into the putrefying porridge below.

Swinging my feet up onto the bridge, I clambered back and lay exhausted on the planks, spitting out the bitter poison. I peered over the edge to see Brimstone thrashing and squelching through the filth before emerging from the mire like a hippopotamus from a swamp. He snorted out a torrent of swill and scrambled on all fours up the slimy bank. He squinted up at me and cursed, as a dollop of excrement slid over his bald head, glistening in the moonlight. I turned and walked away over the bridge, with the biggest smile. By the time I reached the prison wall, I was giggling helplessly.

Much later I sat in Taggi's room, thinking of the fall of Doctor Brimstone and how he'd ripped up only a copy of my father's note rather than the original. I could even feel my father smiling at me and I laughed like never before.

To the coast

—— *Chapter 9* ——

here was something about the graveyard that drew me back. Maybe I needed to keep visiting my grave to make sure it was empty and that I was still alive! But there was something else. That place was where I'd been at my darkest and most despairing. My old self had been buried there but the new me was quite different. I'd discovered something of my past – and that meant I'd discovered part of myself.

From all that I'd learned, I felt stronger and better about who I was – and on top of that I could now start to read, which lifted my self-belief higher than ever before. So I went back to this place of quiet to reflect, to ponder and to look for more clues. The final missing piece of the jigsaw, perhaps.

After a long night of talking with Taggi and laughing so much at 'Brimstone's Bog Dive' as I called it, it was late morning by the time I sat once more by the angel statue among the graves. A warm breeze stirred the leaves as the sun beat down where a shrivelled wreath lay beside a small cross of twigs tied with blue ribbon. It was a wreath lain by an unknown elderly aunt from who knew where? Just maybe she could reveal more to me and shed light into the darkest corners of my past.

I remembered what the old gravedigger had told me about a book inside the church so I crept inside. It was cool and quiet as I stood alone by the altar, staring up at stained-glass windows and beautiful carvings. By the main door, a visitors' book lay on a table, with a quill and a pot of ink. I turned back the pages to see if there were any names like the one Mrs Quilter had told me. There were only a few signatures from the last few weeks and one caught my eye. It simply read Miss Martha Harvey, Blythport.

Hers was the only entry by itself for that week. I felt sure this was the lady I needed to find, but I had no idea how. I walked out into the porch, blinking in the sunlight, and I stood wondering, looking up at the face of the angel.

'Lost?' The old gravedigger was sitting on an upturned barrow, swigging from a hip flask

'Do you happen to know where Blythport is?' I asked.

'Blythport? By the sea, ain't it? Somewhere along the coast road. Not that I've ever been beyond the end of this street. No need when you're blissfully happy, hey?'

He guffawed, threw his head back and almost collapsed in a fit of coughing. With red face and streaming eyes, he took another swig, belched and wiped the back of his hand across his lips.

'Try asking one of the boatmen. They know the coast like their own mothers,' he panted, before stretching out on a slab to bask in the sunshine.

I walked back into the city in the hope of finding someone who would know how I could get to a place I'd never heard of before. At the docks, sailing ships of all sizes were being loaded, unloaded, repaired and secured on moorings with the rise of the tide. Two men were stacking crates in a cart so I asked, 'Can you tell me how to get to Blythport, please?'

'Yeah, just keep rowing,' one of them quipped. His companion pointed to a man harnessing a horse. 'He'll know.' He flung a fish-head to a yapping dog that leapt and caught it in mid-air. I approached the horseman, who was now examining the hooves of his other horse and I asked him the same question. 'Can you tell me how to get to Blythport, please?'

He didn't look up and ignored me completely so I began to walk away.

'Ever scrubbed a carriage?' he called after me. I stared at him, unsure what he meant.

'Lost your tongue? That's a good sign. I can't bear boys what chatter. I leave tomorrow for the north, at sunrise. See that carriage? Make it spotless inside and out, wheels too… you can sit alongside me, so long as you don't talk. We'll pass within ten miles of Blythport sometime the following day. Do a good job and you can sleep in it and guard it tonight while I'm in the ale house. Brushes, buckets, rags and mop in that shed. Spotless, remember. I'm taking gentry tomorrow. Crack of dawn start. Take it or leave it.'

'Thank you,' I said. 'I'll take it, please.'

For the first time, he stopped what he was doing and looked at me. 'I ain't used to pleases and thankyous round here. Are you some sort of gentleman?'

I smiled, went to the shed and was soon setting about cleaning the carriage as best I could. For the rest of the day I washed, scrubbed, brushed and rubbed every part of the wheels, bodywork and seats inside the carriage. 'Not bad,' the man said when the sun was sinking below the rooftops. 'The name's Blake. If anyone needs me I'm in that tavern over the river. Keep an eye on this lot and you'll get your ride to the coast. Let me down and you'll learn that I'm a dab hand with a horsewhip.'

Unsurprisingly, I got little sleep that night, what with the uncomfortable seat to sleep on and all the noises of the docks. Men were loading ships throughout the night and many of them were worse for drink. So, it seemed, was Blake when he appeared before sunrise and began tending the horses, communicating with them and me with nothing more than grunts. One of his guttural noises, accompanied by a gesture, meant I had to sit up at the front of the carriage with him, on a hard bench. I didn't mind for it was high up and, as dawn was breaking, I could see all around as we moved off through the streets to collect four passengers from an inn just outside the city. All day we jolted along through open country, the dust flying in our faces. With fine weather and far views across heathland, I watched country life rolling past from my bouncing seat that threatened to throw me off whenever we hit ruts. At more than one crossroads, gallows stood as a stark reminder to highwaymen – the hanging bodies swinging grotesquely as we rattled past.

Mile after juddering mile we rattled on, the horses sweating and snorting, with Blake saying nothing at all. Only at dusk, as the road finally emerged from a great forest, did we come to a halt by an inn where the passengers disembarked.

'You help me with the horses. We'll pick up new ones in the morning,' was all Blake said.

'How far to Blythport?' I dared to ask.

'Midday tomorrow,' he grunted.

He gave me a tankard of water and a chunk of bread smeared with dripping as I cleaned the carriage once more. That night I had no trouble sleeping inside it, after such a long day on the road. I only hoped, in my last waking moments, that this would all be worth it. After all, there was no guarantee that my only living relative was somewhere ahead, let alone that I would ever find her. I slept, despite draughts and snorting horses, not daring to imagine what the next day might bring.

Rain hammered on the carriage just as the murky light of dawn spilled through the doors, together with water dribbling through the cracks. For a moment, I thought I was already at the coast, for the wind in the trees sounded like the waves I'd heard near the mouth of the river – not that I'd ever seen the proper sea before. As soon as I poked my head out through the door, rain stung my face and the wind buffeted the carriage. The prospects for the journey ahead looked bleak and I braced myself for a day of soakings.

The road, now muddy and full of puddles, slowed our progress and by the time we sloshed to a halt at a desolate crossroads where Blake barked, 'Blythport that way', I was soaked to the skin. An early evening mist rolled across the fields as I clambered down from my perch with a 'Thank you very much, Mr Blake' while one of the passengers shouted at him to speed ahead. So as the carriage splattered off on its way, I was left alone in the clinging mist, with a long walk to the coast ahead of me. The narrow road wound its way through woods before stretching ahead over a heath of gorse bushes and heather. It seemed the bleakest place on earth. After several miles, with my weary feet sloshing through puddles and desolate salt marsh sweeping for miles into the mist, I heard the steady plod and rattle of a horse and cart coming up behind me. A figure in a cap and cape called down to me, 'Want a ride?' He was a boy about my age, whose cart reeked of fish.

'I'm going to Blythport,' I said.

'Now there's a surprise,' he chuckled. 'Seeing as this road goes nowhere else, I didn't think you were heading for the moon!'

I climbed up and sat beside him as the cart juddered on with a swish of the horse's tail.

'Is it far?' I asked.

'Few miles. You're not local then. Running away?'

'No. I'm looking for…' I thought it was worth asking… 'a Miss Harvey. Do you know where she lives by any chance?'

He gave a shrug. 'I only know the fishermen. That's all I do all day, deliver fish. If I was you, I'd ask at the market house. There's a clerk there who knows where everyone lives. He works there every morning.'

'Will he be there now?'

'The town will be dead. Only the taverns are open. You won't find your Miss Harvey tonight.'

I realised what a hopeless wild goose chase this was. I didn't know where I was or where I was going and if I could, I'd have turned around right then and headed back to the city.

'D'you like fish?' the boy asked.

I thought of the fish-head stews Master Groundling made, swimming in onion barley broth.

'Sometimes,' I answered, unconvincingly.

'If you don't mind a bit of mackerel and oat biscuits, you can stay the night with me. It'll be on straw in a fisherman's hut and up at sunrise but you're welcome.'

'Thank you,' I said. Under the circumstances, I couldn't refuse – especially feeling so damp, cold and miserable. So we trundled on towards the sound of waves pounding on shingle, where we eventually drew up by a dilapidated hut on the beach, with fishing boats sprawled around it on the pebbles. With a salty breeze stinging our faces, we unharnessed the horse, tethered it on a tufty patch of grass and entered the hut, steeped in a fishy fug.

'My father used this hut,' the boy said proudly, as if it were a grand palace. 'I came to live here after he drowned and I had to leave the fisherman's cottage up on the cliffs.'

Despite the smell, it was pleasantly warm and dry inside. After lighting a stove on which we cooked a mackerel, we chatted and slumped on straw sacks to the sound of waves washing up the beach and rhythmically shifting shingle. It lulled me into drowsiness... and I slept.

In the silvery light of dawn, the beach rattled to life as boots and boats crunched over stones on all sides of the hut. Men shouted to one another across the shingle as they pulled their boats down to the water's edge and into the surf. The fleet was soon bobbing through the waves, nets being prepared and sails hoisted as they all headed out to the fishing grounds beyond the blurry horizon. I watched them sweeping through the waves from the hut as I chewed on a fishy crust, the sun just breaking through the clouds and gulls wheeling above us.

I thanked my friend, whose name I never knew, for his hospitality, and we parted, him to tend to the horse and cart before the day's catch came in, and me to walk into town in the slender hope of finding the information I was seeking. I could never have imagined how that night on the beach would be the last time I had to sleep in such humble surroundings... for I would never be the same again.

Finding the truth

─── *Chapter 10* ───

The clerk's quill scratched across the page as he perched on a bench behind a high desk piled with leather-bound ledgers.

'Excuse me,' I began, 'can you tell me…'

'Sit. Wait.' He interrupted with a bark that froze my tongue. He didn't look up but continued squinting through his spectacles at the page just inches from his nose. I did as he asked and sat on the only chair in the middle of the otherwise empty room. While I waited, the only sound was the slow scraping of his nib accompanied by his constant sniffing. Not once did the man acknowledge my presence as I waited as patiently as I could. After about half an hour I stood and approached his desk once more, where I cleared my throat and asked...

'I'm looking for a Miss...'

'I said, "Sit". Wait.'

'That's what I've been doing,' I said.

'Then do it some more. You stink of fish.'

'Miss Martha Harvey.' I ignored him by finishing my first sentence as politely as possible.

For the first time, he looked up and stopped writing. 'And what would she have to do with a sprat like you?'

I answered timidly, 'She came looking for me some weeks ago and now I'm looking for her.'

'What is this, some game of hide and seek?' He removed his spectacles and stared at me with a snort.

I continued, 'I just want to know where she lives. Can you tell me, please?'

'She is a lady of learning and I am a man of letters. Neither of us has anything to do with fishy urchins of ill breeding and no culture. Now be gone, muttonhead.'

He picked up his quill but the anger rose in me. I hadn't gone through all this to be insulted and dismissed so rudely.

'I may smell of fish, but I have far more manners than you, for all your letters. For a start, I use a handkerchief instead of sniffing. And just in case you didn't know, that's manners spelt 'M – A - N – N – E – R – S.' I was taught my manners by my father who was a doctor. But seeing as you clearly don't have any manners round here, I am obviously wasting my time.'

I slammed my fist on his desk and the ink pot jumped, almost as high as he did. I was shocked by my own outburst and by the way he sat twitching in front of me, he must have been too. His jaw dropped, as did ink from his nib, splattering across the page.

He sniffed again. 'White house. Large windows. Next but one to the lighthouse.' That was all he said before looking down with horror at the mess in his ledger, scooping it up and scuttling out of the room, muttering obscenities between sniffs.

A church clock struck as I stood by a lighthouse in a narrow street, looking up at a white house surrounded by a low wooden fence. An upstairs window had its curtains drawn across and a wisp of smoke rose from one of the chimneys. I opened the gate, walked up the path and climbed the three steps to the front door to lift a brass lion-head knocker. My hands were sweating and my feet tingled with each clunk. The door was opened by a girl not much older than me, in a starched white apron. 'Tradesmen to the back,' she snapped.

I could see past her into the hallway where a vase of roses stood on a table in front of an ornate looking-glass.

'I wonder if I can speak to Miss Harvey,' I said. The girl eyed me up and down suspiciously. 'She doesn't buy anything from callers. I get her fish from the market.'

'I'm not a trader,' I said. 'I'm… Could you tell her I've come a long way?'

'Name?'

'Er… Angel.' I didn't want to say who I was until I was certain this was the right house. The girl frowned, went back inside and closed the door. After some time, it opened again and I faced a tall, elegant lady in a powder blue dress with white hair tied back in a bun. She stepped out and looked down at me.

'Yes?'

'Are you Miss Harvey?' I asked.

'Indeed.'

'Did you have a relative – called Cornelius or Isabella Catchpole?'

'What do you want?' she asked.

'I think you might know me,' I said.

'I don't think so, dear. I know of no one called Angel.'

'What about Cephas?' I asked.

'Cephas?' She squinted down at me. 'Did you know him?' Her eyes brightened.

'Cephas Catchpole,' I said with a smile.

'How did you know him? Were you friends?' She smiled for the first time.

I offered her my hand. 'So it was you who came to visit the grave. I've found you!'

'Yes, I did. It was very sad. He died just a few days before I arrived. If only…'

I interrupted her. 'Miss Harvey, please listen to me. I have something to tell you. I have some news. Cephas Catchpole is alive.'

For a split second her eyes sparkled hopefully but her expression soon changed.

'Please don't say such things. I have seen his grave.

Poor Cephas died after a sad little life and I regret I never knew that his father died all those years ago. If I had... well, the poor boy might still be alive today.'

'But don't you see, I am!' I couldn't help blurting it out, raising my hands and grinning.

She frowned. 'Tell me your name, dear.'

I took a breath and my words tumbled out in a gabble. 'I'm Cephas Catchpole. My father was Cornelius, a doctor, and my mother was Isabella who went to Australia. I was buried in a coffin but I wasn't dead and I was dug up again. They told me at Brimstone House that you called and I came looking for you.'

She stood perfectly still as if she'd been turned to stone, her hand poised over her mouth.

'Let me look at your face,' she whispered. Her eyes travelled up and down before she said, 'Of course. Those eyes.' She reached out and gently touched my cheek as a tear spilled down her own. Very softly, almost inaudibly, she spoke.

'I think you had better come inside.'

My story took a long time to tell. It began with a sooty coffin and ended in a fishy hut on the beach nearby. Throughout my monologue, Miss Harvey sat almost motionless, absorbing my every word. There were occasional tears, gasps, smiles and sighs. At one point the girl who'd answered the front door appeared at the drawing room door.

'Oh, sorry ma'am, I didn't know the fish boy was still here.'

'He's not the fish boy, May. He's my great nephew. I am thrilled to say I am his Great Aunt Martha.'

Just to hear her say those words filled me with such a feeling of warmth and delight. I actually had an aunt! The girl looked most surprised that, in my filthy, smelly state, I could possibly be related to such an elegant and kind lady.

'Does that mean he's...' Aunt Martha stopped her from saying any more.

'That will be all, thank you, May. Please say nothing of my visitor to anyone.'

'Very well, ma'am,' and the girl hurried from the room.

'I hope you're not ashamed of me,' I said. 'I know I smell and look a mess...'

'My dear,' she laughed, 'I am far from ashamed. I am overjoyed and so proud of you. This news could be the miracle to make all the difference. I just need time to think, that's all. You've taken me so much by surprise, I can't believe it's you. I shall have to keep pinching both of us to make sure we're both real! I want to hear much more about you and I have something to tell you, too. But firstly, you shall have something to eat and a nice hot bath. I shall send May to buy you some clothes and then I will tell you what we need to do. I am so excited!'

She couldn't have been half as excited as I was. There was much I wanted to ask her.

'I have no idea if you are my father's aunt or my mother's. I know nothing about my mother,' I said. 'I'm really hoping you'll be able to tell me something about her. Can you do that, please?'

'Of course, Cephas. You need to know everything. All in good time. In the meantime, I will tell you something else. I will tell you how to find the bath tub.'

By mid-afternoon, I sat in the drawing room, scrubbed clean, smelling more wholesome and dressed in new clothes. Aunt Martha had explained how her dead brother was my grandfather. He died after I was born and before my mother was sent to Australia.

'It must have been terrible when my mother was sent away,' I said. 'I know she wasn't a criminal. All she was doing was trying to take Doctor Brimstone's jar of smallpox to stop him spreading the disease. Doctor Brimstone is a wicked man. He killed my father and he tried to kill me the other night.'

'I know all about him, dear,' she sighed. 'Your poor mother did, too.'

'But do you know when or where she died? No one seems to know exactly. I often wonder if she ever arrived in Australia or if she died on the convict ship.'

'I can tell you exactly,' she said. 'It wasn't on the ship. Your mother was very sick when she arrived in Australia. She was too sick at first to do anything, even to write to your father. No one thought she would survive. But let me tell you something. We Harveys are tougher than people think. Your mother wasn't going to give up without a fight. But by the time she was well enough to write to your father, it was too late. Tragically her first letter arrived the day he died so he never knew what became of her. And she never knew he was in his grave or that you were at the workhouse. It broke her heart not hearing from either of you.'

'Is that what killed her?' I asked, not bearing to hear the answer.

'Almost. But as I say, we Harveys can be tough.'

'So what happened?'

She leaned forward on her chair and put her hand on my knee. 'What I am about to say to you, Cephas, may come as quite a shock. I have waited until now to tell you. Your mother didn't die in Australia as everyone thought she would. She completed her prison sentence by being made to work on an Australian farm… and she finally returned to this country only a few weeks ago.'

I looked her in the eyes and blurted, 'So is she still alive?'

She paused and clasped her hands. 'Yes, dear. She is. But… your mother is very weak. She isn't like she used to be. You see, as soon as she came home, she went straight to your old house. Imagine the bitter blow after waiting so long to see you both again – and the place was in ruins. Her husband was dead and her son was missing, presumed dead. It was the final straw and she gave up all hope. Even her good friend Mr Taggi had disappeared. The poor girl could take no more.'

'Where is she? Where is she now?' I was almost screaming.

Once more she paused and looked down at her hands. 'She is here, dear. Upstairs. I'm looking after her. She came to live here with me. That's when I came to find your graves. She was too distraught to find them herself so I laid wreaths on her behalf. Your mother may come down later. She's not strong enough to be out of bed for long. But when she sees you, I feel sure you will make all the difference. I just think we must break the news to her as gently as we can.'

Without saying a word, I threw my arms around my aunt. There were no words left to say. There were no words to describe my whirlwind of feelings. I wanted to dance, scream and weep all in the same breath. My aunt eventually spoke, my hands in hers.

'I think it would be best if I leave you to tell your mother who you are. Remember she is not well and may be most distressed, but you both need to get to know each other in your own way and in your own time. You, too, may find all this very painful, Cephas, but I can tell you're a thoughtful and sensitive boy. I'm sure you're old enough to understand.'

May stood at the door. 'Please, ma'am, Mrs Catchpole is dressed and ready to come down.'

'In that case,' my aunt said, 'perhaps Cephas would like to go up to meet her and you can both come down together when you are ready.'

I stood immediately and began pacing the room, as nervous as I'd ever been in my life. Just a few minutes ago I had no idea my mother was alive and suddenly I was about to meet her for the first time. Would she be like the picture in my head or would I be disappointed? Would I upset her? Would I be able to cope? Fear, excitement and everything in between rushed through me as I turned to my aunt and stuttered, 'I'm going to try to be brave. After all, I've got a bit of Harvey in me as well, so I've got to be tough.'

'Well done, Cephas,' she beamed. 'You are just like your father, too.'

That was all I needed to hear. Even though my

hands were trembling, I gripped the banister and began to climb the stairs. Incredible as it seemed, I was about to meet my mother... and I was terrified.

Meeting

—— Chapter 11 ——

I stood outside the door for many minutes before taking a deep breath, raising my hand and knocking softly three times. I waited for the woman inside to answer but she didn't. I knocked again: tap… tap… tap… Nothing.

'Open the door and go inside,' my aunt called from the stairs. 'She may be painting. She loses herself in her pictures.'

I did as she said, pushed open the door and

gingerly stepped into the room. Curtains danced in a shaft of sunlight at a large open window. An easel was set in front of it, masking the face of the painter who sat behind. I stood still in the middle of the room, hardly daring to speak but took a breath and croaked, 'Good day.'

Nothing happened. There was no response. I took a step nearer and cleared my throat. 'Good day.'

Very slowly a head moved just slightly from behind the easel but with the light behind her, I couldn't see her face. I waited for a reaction but none came. 'How are you?' I asked, still struggling to know what to say. There was a long pause before a frail voice emerged from the silhouetted face.

'Do I know you?'

I almost gasped aloud as a tingle ran through me. Something deep inside me responded to a long-forgotten tone in her voice.

'Yes,' I tried to answer, though no sound came. A tear snaked down my cheek. I could feel my fingers trembling and my throat was so dry it hurt to speak. After a long silence as I struggled to gain some control, she spoke again in no more than a whisper.

'Who are you?'

Still no words would come. They stuck in my throat and refused to surface. All I could do was stand in front of her and stutter feebly, 'Mother.'

She sat very still, staring at me as I took another step towards her. I so much wanted to see her face and as I drew closer, I could at last glimpse her eyes. It was my turn to stare now. They were eyes I seemed to know. The blurred picture I'd always imagined of my mother's face with deep brown eyes and fair curls was now looking up at me. I couldn't help staring into those troubled eyes with their long lashes and the tiniest flecks of bronze. Once more I tried to speak.

'I'm... I'm...' I felt as if I was being strangled. 'I'm your... son.'

I found myself kneeling at her feet, stretching out my hand to touch her knee. Her eyes were still fixed on where I'd been standing and she murmured, 'I have no son. No one.'

I could hardly see her now, for tears blurred my vision as I struggled to croak, 'I'm Cephas.'

Her face gradually lowered and her eyes descended to look into mine, as she very slowly shook her head. 'No.'

'Yes, really. I'm alive.'

Tears rose in her eyes as she murmured weakly, 'Please don't do this to me.'

I could restrain myself no more. I clung to her and blurted, 'Mother, I've found you!'

As soon as I held her she froze, as if petrified. 'No,' she cried, 'This is wrong. I will be punished again. They will send me away. The heat, the flies, the fear…'

She sat rigid, her face screwed up and her tears running, as if she was in terrible pain.

'It's all right,' I said. 'You're going to be all right now. I'm going to look after you.'

'Please don't let them do this to me. I'm not a criminal, you know.'

I couldn't bear to see her tears and I held her closer to me. There was no response from her other than muffled sobbing. I stroked her cheek and whispered, 'Do you know who I am now?'

She stared at me, trying to concentrate, but her eyes glazed and her brow furrowed, a picture of pathetic despair.

'I don't know what I'm going to do,' she muttered. 'Cornelius would know but he's gone. He took my boy with him. I'll never see them again.'

'But I've come back. I'm your son, Mama. I'm

Cephas. Look, I've grown…'

'They took me away. They wouldn't let me go home. I lost my boys forever.'

'Look, Mama. Do you see this lady?' I showed her my wrist. 'She's looked after me while you've been away. Taggi did this. Do you remember him?' Her eyes suddenly lit up. 'Taggi,' she repeated and for the first time she smiled.

'Mama… You're so lovely when you smile.' I held her hand tightly.

'Taggi loved Cephas,' she said. 'He took him for walks around the garden. You would like Taggi. We all liked Taggi. You would like Cephas.'

'Listen to me, Mama.' I held both her hands. 'Look at me. I am Cephas. It's me. We're together again after all these years and nothing is going to separate us again. Never, I promise.'

She smiled. 'You seem like a nice boy,' she said, 'But you don't live here, do you?'

'I do now. For a while, anyway. With Aunt Martha. This is her house.'

She looked at me indignantly. 'I know that. I'm not stupid, you know.'

'No, Mama, I know. I'm sorry. Shall we go down and see her? We could go out for a walk if you'd like. I've got such a lot to tell you.'

She stood up and looked out of the window, staring at the sea. 'And I can tell you about that ocean. I've been far across it, right across the world, you know. It was terrible.'

She turned back and looked at me. 'Who are you again? Do I know you?'

'Yes, you do. And I'm going to make sure you get to know me a lot more. Come on, Mama… let's go downstairs. Together.'

I held her arm and we slowly walked towards the door. Her skin felt rough and her fingers worn. I looked down to see a black number burnt across the back of her hand.

'My convict number,' she said. 'One day I'm going to show it to Doctor Brimstone and tell him what I think of him.'

'I hope I can be there too,' I said. 'The other night he tried to kill me but he ended up falling in the sewer. He looked like a slimy drowned rat and his face was covered with manure.'

We were at the top of the stairs and she threw her head back and laughed. My aunt rushed into the hallway and looked up at us in disbelief.

'Isabella! She's never laughed before!'

'That, Aunt Martha,' my mother announced haughtily, 'is because I've never before been escorted downstairs by this amusing young man.'

Still amazed, my aunt asked her, 'And do you know who he is?'

She paused and looked at me thoughtfully. 'He said his name is Cephas. The same name as my little son. Isn't that strange?'

She gave a sigh as, arm in arm, we walked down the stairs and out into the sunlit garden.

The next days were difficult and the nights were often worse. I found it hard to sleep and had to keep going to my mother's room, to watch her as she slept, to hear her breathing, to stroke her skin and smell her hair. I would stare at her face for hours. I just wanted to be with her and to assure myself she was alive and well. There were times, when she was awake and at her best, that we could laugh together, but so often she seemed locked in another world from which she couldn't escape.

What I found hardest of all was my mother's confusion. She was unable to realise who I was and that troubled me more than anything. Wonderful though it was to hear her voice, to hold her and see her eyes sparkle, I didn't feel we were getting any closer. She had a coldness about her and I couldn't understand that this was all part of her illness.

A breakthrough came one day on the beach when we were walking at the water's edge in the sunshine. My mother wasn't saying very much and her mood was sombre, when suddenly I saw the boy who'd let me stay in his hut. He was sitting on a shingle bank mending a fishing net. He called over to me, 'Did you find your aunt? Is that her?'

My mother stopped walking and looked at the boy with a pained look on her face. She took me by the hand and led me to him. 'This is Cephas,' she said. 'I'm not his aunt… I'm his mother, you know.'

At that moment, it was as if a dark cloud lifted from her. She whimpered before dropping to her knees, pulling me close and sobbing like never before. The boy sat quite dumbfounded as we cried, with my mother saying over and over again, 'You're my son! You're my son!'

From then on, it was me who was watched at night. I would often wake to see my mother sitting with a candle at my bedside. She would be watching me, smiling and saying my name. Sometimes she was telling me about my father or describing her time in Australia. She spoke of our home just after I was born, and how she feared Doctor Brimstone was keeping jars of smallpox so he could spread the disease and make money from his useless medicine. She sobbed as she described being sentenced in court and being bundled onto the convict ship.

'It was the price I paid for trying to do the right thing. I'm so sorry I failed you, Cephas.'

'You and father were very brave,' I said. 'And I'm so proud of you.'

She kissed my forehead. She knew I meant it and her tears were proof that she was at last somewhere on the road to recovery.

Each day my mother grew stronger and, as we walked along the cliffs every morning, she would ask me more about my own story, talking less of her feelings of guilt. Slowly, as she let go of her anguish of the past eight years, she took a greater interest in the world around her. Her paintings, once dark and menacing, became brighter and full of colour.

One afternoon, as I wrote to Edith to tell her

my incredible news, my mother said, 'Why don't we both write down our stories for each other? They will help us unlock all that's inside us and we'll both get to understand one another better.'

'A good idea,' I said. 'But you'll have to help me with spelling. I'm not very good at writing.'

That evening I began the difficult task of trying to write down how I came to discover who I was. The nib scratched over the paper as I started to write my story.

Never having written much before, my hand was unsteady as I tried to grip the quill and shape letters into meaningful words. I wasn't sure where to begin but once more my mind was drawn back to the graveyard, as my first sentence slowly stretched across the page:

Being dead came as a terrible surprise...

Sentenced to hang

—— *Chapter 12* ——

Dear Cephas,

Thank you for your letter which I was very thrilled to open. It was the first letter I have ever received. You can imagine what a fuss it caused here when it arrived but with father out of the way (I will tell you why soon) your letter came to me with the seal unbroken. I was very proud of your writing – you must have had an excellent teacher!

I am so pleased for you that you found your aunt's house and the special one you discovered there. What a wonderful piece to your jigsaw. I told you *that you would soon build up the whole picture. You must be overjoyed. I am very happy for you. But Cephas, you cannot imagine how I miss you. It has been such a long time that you have been away. When are you coming back to see me? Mother keeps asking about you.*

That night I last saw you when you and Mr Cutpurse and Mr Dalrymple visited father seems so long ago now. Father got home late that night and he was in such a foul temper. What you all said to him made him wild. I have never known him to be so angry. He was also in a disgusting state and smelling most putrid. It was only later I learned what had happened. I did smile, although the results of that night are likely to be serious in many ways.

I am still getting in and out of the house through my window so I can get to see mother whenever I like now. I do not have to worry about Mrs Quilter as she is always busy looking after father. He is very ill and stays in bed all day in his room. Mother and I are not allowed to see him – not that we mind about that. Mrs Quilter says he is in a bad way after falling in the sewer and breathing in all the bad air. He has some sort of disease and nothing is making him better. The other doctors do not come to see him any more. They said they had done all they could for him. Mrs Quilter cries a lot and says he might die soon and the only thing keeping him alive is the big day next week. He is clinging on to hear the news.

There are going to be crowds in the streets and great gatherings in the city next Friday to mark the King's anniversary. There will be fireworks, beacons lit, street parties, music parades and many celebrations. But father is not excited about any of those. The only thing keeping him alive is hearing in the evening that two people have been executed. You see, Cephas, I am very sad to tell you that his last influence on this world will be on Jack Cutpurse and Horace Dalrymple. They are both to hang late afternoon next Friday. Father was responsible for having them sentenced to death for grave-robbing and smuggling. I know they had done wrong in many ways but father made up all kinds of stories to seek his revenge on them. Because of all his money and power in the city, the judge believed his every word. Their execution will bring a bigger crowd than ever as it starts the weekend of celebrations for the King. I know you will be upset to hear this news, just as I was. Mrs Quilter is to witness the hanging on his

155

behalf before going straight back to his bedside to describe it to him, so they can drink a toast to 'dead enemies'. I think it is all terrible and again I am so ashamed of father for his cruelty. Nothing will change him and it saddens me so much. When I think of all the misery he caused your family I still weep for you. My poor mother does, too. If my father dies, I think she will feel great relief to be free. I know that must sound terrible but for years we have been prisoners here and are always afraid of his violent rages.

Just before the men's trial, Mrs Dalrymple appeared at our door. She was demanding to speak to my father but he was already very ill and he could not see her. Mrs Quilter would not let her in the door and you can imagine what a terrible catfight they had. Josiah had to come with a garden fork to keep the women from scratching each other apart. I could hear the squealing and wailing from my room. The only good thing about it all was that she had Tooth with her so he had been let out of the smallpox hospital at last. He was lucky to survive and Mrs Quilter said he was badly pockmarked. Mind you, she used quite a few other words to describe him! Sadly, Lotty died from smallpox, *so Mrs Dalrymple was very distressed at losing a daughter and shortly her husband. It must be a worrying time for her and Tooth. What will happen to them after the two men are hanged? They will not be able to pay the rent and will have nowhere to live. Mother says we will also be homeless when father dies. He has already told her that he has written in his will that he is leaving the house to Mrs Quilter. We may not get a penny.*

So, with one thing and another, it is all bad news – apart from your own, of course. I only hope you can both come and see me before too long. It would be so good to ride out in the cart with Josiah again. We could go anywhere you like.

I expect that a report of the hanging will appear in the newspaper. I shall cut it out and send it to you – not that you will want to read it, I know.
I hope you will write back to me soon.

Your good friend,

Edith

I read the letter many times before going into my mother's room. She was sitting by the window, humming to herself as she painted. A sea breeze rippled the curtains and ruffled her curls. She looked up, alert now and with a real glow to her cheeks.

'Mama, I've got an idea. Why don't we go away for a few days? We can go to the city. It will do you good to visit old friends and see some familiar places again. There's someone we both need to see. Not only that, there's something really important I need to do.'

She grinned. 'Of course. Just what the doctor ordered!'

The Final Twist

Chapter 13

DAILY GAZETTE

25TH OCTOBER

CELEBRATIONS AND EXECUTIONS

The streets of the city have been full of our cheering populace during the last days and nights. With the anniversary of our Monarch's accession to the Throne, all taverns and inns have been most full, with much merriment abroad. A great number of children belonging to the workhouses appeared at the City Hall at daybreak, and a youth made a handsome speech about His Majesty. There was the greatest joy and magnificence that it was possible for loyal subjects to shew to their most Gracious Sovereign.

At noon, all guns along the river will be discharged, followed by a fine display of soldiery and the sound of musical instruments. In the evening, fireworks will be lighted, with great bonfires of pitch barrels; the streets to be illuminated, with all manner of demonstrations of public joy.

In the courtyard of the prison, extra executions are set up for the entertainment of the crowds. One such is most worthy of note for being unheard of in the history of the city. Two felons guilty of stealing from churchyards and smuggling contraband from the docks will be brought before the gallows shortly before sunset. Jack Cutpurse and Horace Dalrymple are to perish in unison from adjacent nooses at the hands of the famous hangman Titus Twist, of great popularity with the masses.

Although I vowed never to return to the dreaded scene of execution in the prison yard, I found myself back there in the late afternoon sunshine of autumn, clinging to the top of the prison gates with a hideous view of the scaffold. All around were vast crowds in buoyant mood awaiting a double hanging of grave-robbers – a spectacle that none could resist. The sense of expectation was mounting around me, while I could only cling uncomfortably as nervousness churned inside me like a bundle of wriggling snakes.

As soon as a bell began to toll and the horse pulling the prisoners' cart snorted below me as it entered the yard, a deafening cheer rose from the crowd. Like a returning nightmare, the scene made me sweat and tremble as hats were thrown, handkerchiefs waved and kisses blown. When the two prisoners came into view, everyone roared, whistled and whooped, followed by a slow hand-clap as the cart slowly arrived at the platform where two nooses swung in the breeze.

Unable to look at Jack Cutpurse and Horace Dalrymple as they were wheeled towards the gallows, I instead glanced down to a cart with two horses drawing up below me just outside the prison gates. The coachman and his female companion sat very still, both draped in blankets, with eyes fixed on the road ahead.

At a sudden cheer rising from the crowds, I looked back to the gallows where a cloaked and hooded figure in black appeared behind the platform. The hangman slowly ascended the steps and stood totally still with arms folded, the only movement being the stirring of his cloak in the breeze. Everyone watched the agonisingly slow edging of the cart into position beneath the two nooses. With wrists tied behind their backs, the two stooped prisoners looked out pathetically at the jeering mob. The hangman stepped forward and, to much applause, he twisted each noose before placing them under the chins of the terrified prisoners. He then tightened them around the throats of each man, facing the heckling rabble.

Titus the Rope stood motionless, his head turned towards the horseman sitting very still at the front of the prisoners' cart, holding the reins. Slowly raising his arm and pointing a steady finger at the horseman, the hangman held his pose for a few seconds as a breathless hush descended. In that silence, it was possible to hear a bead of sweat drop.

Nothing stirred, as all eyes fixed on the quivering prisoners – until heads turned towards a noisy disturbance just in front of the horse, where a boy darted from the crowd, waving a purse. A screaming woman chased him, hollering she'd been robbed. The horse reared, the hangman shouted 'pickpocket' and pointed accusingly at the boy running towards the gates. All eyes followed him, as constables ran out from all directions. Amid the commotion, all attention to the gallows was momentarily distracted. Few people, apart from me, noticed the hangman jump onto the cart and pull a knife from his cloak. He cut down both prisoners and all three dropped to their knees inside the cart. The hangman kicked the horseman off his seat into the mud and grabbed the reins. The cart lurched forward, spun round and sped towards the prison gates in a spray of sand but turned so sharply right in front of me that the whole cart tipped up on two wheels. The three men jumped clear and disappeared through the gates just as the cart crashed on its side with an almighty crack and billowing clouds of dust. With wheels still spinning and horse staggering to its feet, the cart completely blocked the exit so that charging soldiers on horseback were unable to get through and make chase. In case they did, I'd already jumped to the ground outside and pulled the huge gates shut, even though other spectators were clinging to them and cursing me, spitting down on my head.

Outside the gates, I leapt onto the waiting cart where Josiah and my mother sat with a new cargo of the three men, the boy with the purse and the woman who had chased him (Tooth and Mrs Dalrymple). As soon as we all landed in the back, Josiah cracked his whip and his horses sprang forward. We clattered off at breath-taking speed while my mother threw a large bed sheet over us to ensure no one saw what was being whisked away through the city.

The horses charged down narrow streets, round tight bends, over crossroads and through archways, the cart's wheels roaring over the cobbles as crowds scattered before us – parting like the bow-waves from a ship. After racing down an alleyway only just wide enough, Josiah wrenched the reins, swung the cart between the pillars of a portico and juddered to a halt in a back yard.

'We've done it,' my mother shouted. 'Titus has saved the day!' She pulled back the sheet and we cheered before clambering from the cart, all shaking hands and patting each other's backs.

'Angel, you are nothing short of a genius for arranging all this. We can never thank you enough.' Jack was close to tears as he shook me firmly by the hand. The cut noose still dangled from his neck.

'I'm just paying you both back for saving me from the grave one night,' I grinned back at him.

'The best thing we ever did,' Horace wheezed, his hand on my shoulder.

'I'd give five shillings to see the look on Brimstone's face right now,' Mrs Dalrymple cackled. 'When he hears you've escaped, he's likely to self-combust.'

'It'll kill him,' Tooth squealed, 'and good riddance if yer ask me. Good luck, Angel.'

'Good luck to you all,' my mother called above the noise of soldiers' horses racing past. By now the cart and driver were well disguised with fresh covers and clothes.

'And our thanks again to you, Mister Hangman. I never thought I'd meet Titus the Rope face to face.' Jack shook Taggi by the hand.

'All part of the service,' he replied, before climbing back up into the cart. 'Forgive me, but I must hurry. My ship leaves within the hour. God's speed to you all.'

My mother and I joined Taggi in the cart as he threw his hood and cloak to Tooth. 'Have this, my friend. I have no need for it now.'

The four of them waved, with broad smiles as we moved off. They scuttled down an alley just as a line of constables marched down the street. A few of them glanced at us ambling along and decided we looked nothing like the cart and its fugitive occupants they were pursuing.

'We are so grateful to you for helping everyone, Taggi,' my mother said. 'It was wonderful to spend these last days with you. I'm just so sad you've got to run away like this now.'

'Not at all,' Taggi answered calmly. 'For years I have longed to return home and I never had the courage to make a run for it on my own. You have helped me on my way. I am thrilled to be heading for India at last. I am thrilled, too, we had the chance to meet again and to see you reunited with dear Cephas. Cornelius would be so proud.'

'We need to hurry,' I called to Josiah. 'Taggi's ship sails very soon. The sun is already setting.'

'Very well, Master Catchpole. Happy to oblige.'

Josiah rattled the reins and the horses trotted on towards the docks. A red sky smouldered behind us and the first fireworks of the evening celebrations crackled above. We passed crowds milling towards us, making their way to the lighting of the bonfires.

'You look very serious, Taggi,' my mother said, touching his hand.

'I am just thinking, Isabella. There will be many changes for us in the months ahead. Much has happened lately and we must each decide about where to live and what to do. It's just like a saying we have back home which means something like 'however many twists and turns our lives may take, everything unravels in the end'. And like a noose, that can be in the very last seconds… when I've always made a prayer that the unravelling brings final peace.'

'I don't know about unravelling ropes, I just hope I don't have many more missing pieces in my jigsaw!' I smiled, holding out my hand to shake his. He took my wrist and kissed 'My Lady' who looked up at him as he smiled.

'I have your last missing piece, Cephas,' my mother said thoughtfully. 'Hearing those fireworks has reminded me of a time of great happiness in the past. I last heard them eleven years ago. It was the night I gave birth to the sweetest baby boy. This night must be your birthday, my love!'

I hugged her as the cart rumbled down to the docks, past an assortment of bobbing boats on the rising tide, until we stopped beside a tall sailing ship, its masts and rigging towering above us. Sailors scurried on deck in its final minutes before sailing. We stepped down from the cart onto the quayside. Taggi graciously bowed, his hands together with fingertips to his nose, before embracing my mother. Speaking very softly, his voice cracking with emotion, he held us both. 'I hope it will not be long before you both make the journey to come and see me.'

There was no time to answer. Suddenly the clattering of soldier's horses echoed around us in a terrifying jangle of brass and swishing swords.

'Quick, Taggi, get on board,' my mother pleaded, pushing him towards the ship, where ropes were being untied and swiftly thrown. He ran up the gangplank, jumped on deck just in time, turned and raised his hand, as the anchor began to rise. Very slowly the sails filled and the ship edged away from the quay.

'Have you seen anyone run aboard any of these ships, ma'am?' a soldier called to my mother, his voice brisk and urgent.

'Only the innocent,' she said.

'But what of a cloaked and hooded figure?' he barked.

I answered calmly, 'We've seen no one like that here. Can you tell us who he is?'

'That's the mystery; no one knows what the rapscallion looks like. Sorry to startle you, ma'am. It looks like that Indian gentleman wants your attention.'

The soldiers swirled away in a ricochet of shouts and galloping hooves – off to search a fishing boat upriver for a villainous stowaway - as we turned with relief to watch the dignified figure still waving from the quarterdeck. All we could see, as the ship sailed majestically into the estuary towards the rising moon, was Taggi's shining smile. We stood watching as the darkness descended and touched the misty water, while behind us the blazing bonfires lit up the entire city and singed the sky. I held my mother's hand and quietly sighed when, at last, the disappearing sails were swallowed by the night.

My mother looked down at me, squeezed my fingers and smiled, as the dancing flames reflected off the fiery water of the dock and sparked in her eyes. It was then I turned my back on the moon and the great sweep of impenetrable darkness… to head, like a moth emerging at last from its chrysalis, towards the beckoning light.

THE END

Postscript

I couldn't believe it. On my first day of training as a doctor at the hospital, who should my first patient be? He had a cluster of unsavoury boils bubbling up on his rear end. He was a certain Artimus Groundling who, needless to say, had no idea who his trainee boil-lancer happened to be. I recognised the smell of soot, gin and onions and performed the operation swiftly, effectively and with just the hint of a smile. I didn't say a word – as he wailed like an infant.

Cephas Catchpole

P.S. As I began to write my complete story, having at last the privilege of receiving some education, I became engaged to Edith Brimstone.

She is as much part of my journey from darkness into light as anyone, and I shall always be grateful for her loyal belief in me, despite my many frailties.

'Ignorance, like disease, can only be conquered by the tireless endeavours of the wise.

If we are any less ignorant, more civilised or healthier now than in the past, we have education, science and books to thank. All three are as vital today as ever to the future of civilisation… and to slaying the monsters that curse, scare, divide and threaten us.'

Edith Catchpole
(eulogy to Doctor Cephas Catchpole, 1868)

Key dates behind Cephas Catchpole's story and beyond...

1400–1800 Over 500,000 smallpox-related deaths occur in Europe each year.

1751 In London a record 3,538 smallpox deaths for the year are recorded.

1787 Transportation – the first fleet sails to Australia, taking 736 convicts.

1796 Edward Jenner develops a method to protect people from smallpox by giving them cowpox virus. He rubs pus from a dairymaid's cowpox pustule into scratches on the arm of his gardener's eight-year-old son (James Phipps), and then exposes him to smallpox six weeks later. Success! The process becomes known as vaccination, from the Latin *vacca* for cow. Scientists at the time thought Jenner out of his mind.

1808   End of the death penalty for pickpockets in UK.

1820   Law passed stopping flogging of women in prison in UK. Over 200 offences can be punished by hanging.

1829   Over 25,000 people attend and cheer the hanging of William Burke in Edinburgh. He and William Hare were notorious body-snatchers or 'resurrectionists' who robbed graves and murdered to supply doctors with fresh corpses to dissect. The first real police force in England is started – 1,000 police officers based at Scotland Yard, London.

1844   First experiments with anaesthetics. Dr Horace Wells, American dentist, uses nitrous oxide as an anaesthetic (unsuccessfully).

1846   Boston dentist Dr William Morton successfully demonstrates ether's anaesthetic properties during a public tooth extraction.

1853   Vaccination with cowpox is made compulsory in Britain.

1865   The first woman doctor qualifies in Britain (ten years after the first woman surgeon in the United States).

1867   Joseph Lister publishes 'Antiseptic Principle of the Practice of Surgery', one of the most important developments in medicine. Lister stressed the need for cleanliness in operations, a revolutionary idea at the time.

1868   The last time someone is hanged in public in England.

1870   Elementary Education Act 1870: compulsory education for all children aged 5–13 in England and Wales.

1872   The use of the stocks as a punishment is stopped in England.

1900–1980 An estimated 300 million people die from smallpox around the world.

1936   Last public hanging in the United States.

1962   Smallpox outbreak in South Wales (approximately 20 deaths).

1964   The last time someone is hanged in prison in England.

1974   Smallpox epidemic in India (15,000 deaths).

1980   WHO (World Health Organisation) announces smallpox is eradicated. After 180 years of vaccinations, smallpox is at last wiped out. The curse of the dreaded 'speckled monster' is over forever.

1992   The last hangman in Britain dies.

2020s   The final eradication of polio after decades of vaccination?

GLOSSARY

Digitalis
A powerful drug used to stimulate the heart and made from the dried leaves of the foxglove – highly poisonous in certain doses.

Dropsy
A term once used for a condition when fluid built up in the body such as under the skin or in the legs, leading to swelling and discomfort.

Foundling
A very young child or baby found after being abandoned by unknown parents.

Malevolent
Wanting to bring harm or evil to others.

Opium
A bitter brownish drug (used in morphine as a painkiller) made from the dried juice of the opium poppy.

Portico

A row of columns supporting a roof around the entrance of a building.

Pustule

A small inflamed bump or blister of the skin filled with pus.

Reprobate

A wicked person and a criminal.

Vaccination

Injection of a killed microbe or weak virus to stimulate the immune system into protecting the body against a disease.

Workhouse

An institution in which the needy people of a parish received board and lodging in return for work. In Britain, in the 17th to 19th centuries, a workhouse was often a severe place where the poorest could live and do unpleasant jobs in return for food and accommodation.

A selected list of Scribo titles

The prices shown below are correct at the time of going to press. However, The Salariya Book Company reserves the right to show new retail prices on covers, which may differ from those previously advertised.

The Long-Lost Secret Diary
of the World's Worst... by Tim Collins

Knight	978-1-912006-67-0	£6.99
Pirate	978-1-912006-66-3	£6.99
Astronaut	978-1-912233-20-5	£6.99
Dinosaur Hunter	978-1-912233-19-9	£6.99

Gladiator School by Dan Scott

1 Blood Oath	978-1-908177-48-3	£6.99
2 Blood & Fire	978-1-908973-60-3	£6.99
3 Blood & Sand	978-1-909645-16-5	£6.99
4 Blood Vengeance	978-1-909645-62-2	£6.99
5 Blood & Thunder	978-1-910184-20-2	£6.99
6 Blood Justice	978-1-910184-43-1	£6.99

Iron Sky by Alex Woolf

1 Dread Eagle	978-1-909645-00-4	£9.99
2 Call of the Phoenix	978-1-910184-87-5	£6.99

Children of the Nile by Alain Surget

1 Cleopatra must be Saved!	978-1-907184-73-4	£5.99
2 Caesar, Who's he?	978-1-907184-74-1	£5.99
3 Prisoners in the Pyramid	978-1-909645-59-2	£5.99
4 Danger at the Circus!	978-1-909645-60-8	£5.99

Ballet School by Fiona Macdonald

1. Peter & The Wolf	978-1-911242-37-6	£6.99
2. Samira's Garden	978-1-912006-62-5	£6.99

Aldo Moon by Alex Woolf

Aldo Moon and the Ghost at Gravewood Hall	978-1-908177-84-1	£6.99

The Shakespeare Plot by Alex Woolf

1 Assassin's Code	978-1-911242-38-3	£9.99
2 The Dark Forest	978-1-912006-95-3	£9.99
3 The Powder Treason	978-1-912006-33-5	£9.99

All Scribo and Salariya Book Company titles can be ordered from your local bookshop, or by post from:

The Salariya Book Co. Ltd,

25 Marlborough Place

Brighton

BN1 1UB